Chakra Secrets

On the Path to Love and Happiness

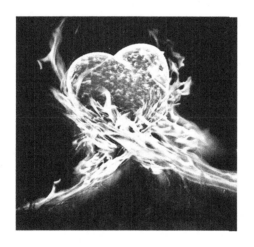

Becca Chopra

For information, address Creative Counsel, RR2 Box 3902, Pahoa, HI 96778, or visit www.TheChakras.org.

FIRST EDITION

Cover Design by Indie Author Services. Photography by Naia Rae Fox; Photoshop by Joseph Doherty.

ISBN-13: 978-1478169918
ISBN-10: 1478169915

*Dedicated to all the wounded healers,
who discover the healing power of love
and share it with the world.*

Inspired by J. S., my best friend forever.

ALSO BY BECCA CHOPRA:

The Chakra Diaries
Balance your Chakras, Balance your Life with Dynamind
Balance and Tone your Chakras DVD

Chakra Secrets

On the Path to Love and Happiness

CONTENTS

Author's Note

MY PATH & YOUR PATH

"As you start to walk out on the way,
the way appears."
~ Rumi

Saint or sinner? Could I possibly lift myself off the pavement, where I literally lay deep in a well of grief and guilt, a self-absorbed actor and widow? And move into the light as a respected energy healer and yoga teacher? Or would bad decisions and betrayals, in the past and even in my past lives, block my way?

Part I of this book is my personal story, in which yoga, meditation, tantric studies and Huna all propel me forward.

I've been revered by some, condemned as a tantric temptress and man-grabbing guru by others. Granted, I overstepped the boundaries between teacher and student, between friends, but maybe I can feel forgiveness after all my secrets are revealed.

Part II contains the instant healing secret I ultimately learned. It can help you on your path. Use it daily or whenever you have pain – physical, emotional, mental or spiritual. It will help you to balance your chakras, to jump over any hurdles in your life, to more quickly find your balance, your healing, your happiness.

Balance your chakras, balance your life!

Namaste,
Becca Chopra

PART 1

My Path

*"Praise and blame, gain and loss,
pleasure and sorrow
come and go like the wind.
To be happy, rest like a giant tree,
in the midst of them all."*

~ The Buddha

From Stage to Scream

"Let's not forget that the little emotions are the great captains of our lives and we obey them without realizing it."

~ Vincent Van Gogh

The champagne cork flew across the dimly-lit, cramped closet that served as my dressing room, crashing into the mirror where I scared myself with my own scowl.

"What's to celebrate? Closing on opening night?" I cried, dripping with champagne and sweat. We didn't have to wait for the reviews to come in, we had heard the weak applause from the audience as they rushed from the half-empty seats at the end of the show.

"Chill, Rebecca," said Richard, my partner in drama and in life, as he poured with the steady hand of a long-time alcoholic, getting nary a drop on himself. Mr. Cool. "C'mon, have a drink and powder that cute little nose," he said as he laid out another line of coke. "It's cast party time. You were great, by the way," he said, sliding a compliment in the back door before slamming it in my face as usual.

"Well, you might have been too if you weren't so coked up," I said, wondering how he could still be so high on life after our dismal failure. His sweet talk and smoothness gave me a split-second cellular memory of how it used to be between us, when I thought we were held together by love, not codependency.

We were part of *The Chakra Monologues* cast, playing out the emotions of the rainbow-colored energy centers of the body. Richard appropriately played the center of confidence and energy, the yellow Solar Plexus Chakra, although after tonight it might be renamed the Coke Chakra. He had raced through his

3

lines, all over the place and everywhere at once. When the spotlight turned green for me, my cue as the Heart Chakra, I was fuming and fudged my time in the limelight, tripping over my own tongue. I was supposed to be green with love, not with bile.

"Richard, you screwed it up, admit it."

"Bitch, bitch, bitch, that's all you ever do. Bitch, bitch, bitch," he said, as he laid out yet another line. "You wrote a good script babe, but the only character the audience really cared about was the sexy Sacral Chakra."

Well, sexy Sacral had obviously entranced him.

My only reason for staying with Richard – to launch the play with his connections, hoping it would connect *us* again – was now a moot point. The curtain had now fallen not only on our play but also on our six-year relationship, starting with a whirlwind college romance, ending in a disintegrating marriage.

Celebrate? I threw the long-stemmed crystal at the wall, picking up a shard. I wanted to cut the cord that attached me to him for better or worse. But I wearily dropped the crystal blade in the rubbish instead.

"FYI, I'm getting a ride with Denise, the only woman in the cast and crew I'm sure you haven't slept with!" My voice quaked, my angry and broken Heart Chakra spinning out of control. "I'm leaving before I kill you."

His deep baritone called, "Doll, wait a holy minute," but I was already closing the door on this storybook romance with an unhappy ending. I didn't want to be with him a second longer.

I cried all the way to Club Zero. But when Denise pulled

up to the neon-lighted entrance, my actor's training bobbed to the surface, and I painted on a false smile and joined the rest of the cast. The club was so crowded that our rainbow outfits were the only blotches of color in a black haze of dripping mascara, bouncing bodies, and pointy-toed shoes dancing to ear-blasting techno pop.

The director and producer weren't there – they must have slunk away fast to lick their wounds and count their leftover change.

I threw myself headlong into the mass mayhem, trying to shake off my misery. Before I knew it, I was dressed in black too, my green-as-grass Heart Chakra dress soaked through with gallons of more sweat and cheap champagne.

The clock struck closing time and my heart, amazingly to me, skipped a beat, still hoping my once-Prince Charming would show up as the person I had loved so blindly, so single-mindedly. But no fairy tale here, no Richard, no hero, no footman, no golden carriage arrived at Club Zero. Of course, neither had Susan, Ms. Sexy Chakra to Richard.

I knew I should ask for a divorce – the only option that wouldn't land me behind bars.

Suddenly a cool breeze wafted through the thick stink of the club as I visualized myself alone in our apartment in the Hollywood Hills. Enough closet space for once. No toilet seat left up. No husband stumbling home at dawn with morning breath fierce enough to straighten Whoopi Goldberg's hair.

I admit, the thought of divorcing Richard – my soul mate, the person I recognized the instant I saw him as the love of my life – cut me to the very core. But he had changed into someone I barely recognized.

Needing to lash out against somebody or something, I smashed another champagne glass, this time on the marble floor of the dance club, and announced to no one in particular that I was giving up acting and giving up on love.

But Denise heard me. She played the Crown Chakra, or spiritual chakra in the cast. Still beautiful in her balloon burst of violet satin, she pried me up, up and away, off the padded banquet where my sticky dress and sad-sack soul had become glued.

"C'mon, let's get out of here," she said. "There are better men and better parts waiting for us."

"Maybe for you."

"C'mon, I'm taking you home," Denise insisted.

I blew a farewell kiss toward the room, taking my final curtain call, leaving my bright hopes and dreams of Hollywood behind.

Just a few blocks from the club, red lights were flashing and sirens screeched. "Must be an accident," Denise mumbled. Suddenly sober, I knew. Before we even saw his crumpled, broken yellow Porsche, I knew it was Richard.

I didn't have to do the deed myself, after all.

Jesus, what was I thinking?

The police vainly tried to stop me with barricades and brawny blue arms, but they were no match for my superpower of guilt. I crawled my way around and under to where the paramedics were working. I looked toward heaven as I began to pray, but then I saw it was too late for prayers.

Susan was on one stretcher, my Richard on the other. Looking nothing like the model on the Calvin Klein billboard right above him, the one that had been his star vehicle. There, he still wore his beatific smile as if he really believed that "Citrus Spritz makes you happier, more alert, and definitely irresistible." I stood frozen at the horror of the actual here and now, then melted like the smoldering rubber and metal on the grimy asphalt.

Was this a nightmare, like the many I'd screamed through since meeting Richard? I felt woozy and woozier as the curtain came down.

I opened my eyes as paramedics roughly covered my face with an oxygen mask and I found myself staring right up at that billboard. Richard's eyes said, "It's your fault, Rebecca. You stopped loving me. You pushed me away. You directed my self-destruction."

Barely Breathing

"You can bear anything, if it isn't your own fault."

~ Katherine Fullerton

"Breathe in the light. Breathe out the guilt," said the gray-haired therapist in the gray silk suit. Her soothing, sweet-as-mother's-milk voice reminded me of all the New Age meditation tapes I had listened to over the last six months since the accident, over and over and over again to no avail.

"You're wallowing in it," she said. "It's time to let it go. You're not ALL POWERFUL! You didn't cause Richard's accident just because you said you wanted him dead."

Oh, yeah?

"Just telling me that doesn't help," I said.

"Well, talk to me. Where did you get this grandiose idea you could kill someone with your emotions?"

"Talking doesn't help."

"Rebecca, tell me, when did you first get this feeling that your thoughts, your anger, could actually kill another person?"

"Well, I don't think I ever really knew it until now. But as a child, I often got mad at my mother and would give her the silent treatment. But she wouldn't let me go to bed without saying, 'Now, give me a kiss, dear. If I die in my sleep, you'll be sorry.'

"I would give in, even if I didn't want to. Then I'd be so relieved when I woke up to the smell of her French toast the next morning."

I don't think the therapist had ever heard anything so

convoluted, but she probably wasn't brought up Catholic. She furrowed her brow, crossed her legs, took a sip of tea, tapped finger after finger on her bright red lipstick and asked, "You were what, 4, 5, 6 years old?"

"About that."

"Let's do some inner child work and strip out the false notion that your anger could kill someone."

"Oh, let's not," I begged, hiding my head in her pillow. Hearing the clock tick, I finally decided to face the music, peeked over the pillow and asked, "How do I clear my *adult* mind of guilt? I stopped loving Richard. I stopped giving him the adoration he needed. The adoration I had given him for so long. I'm to blame. Maybe all actors die when their fans desert them."

"Rebecca, we need to dissolve the root cause of your guilt before it makes you really sick. The feeling of guilt is like sipping a bit of poison every day."

"I really don't feel my Mother's notion of Catholic guilt is why I'm overwhelmed now. I've lost my husband, for God's sake! I feel I could have done something differently. I was meant to be with Richard. I always knew it."

"Obviously you were wrong. What made you think he was your soul mate?"

"I didn't think it, I felt it."

"Well, think about it. Think of your choices – past and present. Our time is up for today. Let's talk about it more next week. Now, be sure to get some sleep."

I couldn't. I had lain awake for the last six months, and I

lay awake for seven nights more, going over the last six years, trying to frame an answer to her question. That gut feeling that Richard and I were soul mates – had I been dead wrong?

Dredging Up the Past

"Life is the sum of all your choices."

~ Albert Camus

Whom it came to love at first sight, I had always been
an atheist, but the night I met Richard, I became an
instant convert.

*Hey, I know you. Your face is a bright memory from a
hazy, hazy past.*

So many things had changed since he transferred to Yale
that stormy fall and his commanding King Lear electrified our
stage with his voice booming, "Dear Maiden, thy horn is dry."

I had heard everyone excitedly gossip about him before
I saw his face up close at our drama department's Christmas
party. I took one look at him and thought, *This is it. I know him.
He belongs to me.*

When he coolly, casually pushed up his cashmere sleeves
at the sweltering party full of theatrically gesturing students,
the golden brown hair on his forearms glistened familiarly. The
rest of him was even more captivating, exploding my heart with
passion it had never felt before in my 19 years, not even while
playing Juliet freshman year.

I was mesmerized – I stared at him until he felt my gaze,
a fiery gaze intent on getting him to notice me too, a gaze that
didn't waver even when he stared back with question marks
shooting out of his big baby blues. I didn't dare blink for fear of
breaking the spell, the connection.

He finally walked over and asked, "Shall we dance or just
stare all night?"

I swallowed my embarrassment and just took his hand and moved onto the parquet dance floor to that sappy yet now suddenly appropriate slow song, "Endless Love."

His touch made every cell in my body tremble, but his arms held me tightly, like they would keep me safe and never let me go. It seemed unbelievable for a first dance, but I knew I had been here, done this before, and I was back for more.

He broke the ice whispering a Shakespeare sonnet in my ear.

His cool, charming manner relaxed me, as did the delicious citrus scent of his neck as I laid my head on his shoulder when the DJ put on Whitney Houston's "I Will Always Love You."

"Let's go somewhere less noisy," he said, when Whitney was replaced with Guns N' Roses.

I followed in a semi-drunk, starry-eyed daze across the college green, then through town, barely noticing the gusts of freezing rain, to his off-campus apartment.

So, he wasn't a scholarship student like me, but a rich kid....

Soaked and chilled on the outside but flushed with sizzling infatuation, I snuggled into the navy fleece robe hanging in his bathroom and dabbed some of his Calvin Klein Citrus Spritz behind my ears as he set up the ebony and ivory chess board.

We played three games of chess, drank cup after cup of steaming coffee laced with Irish whiskey, and shared kiss after steamy kiss between moves. Richard expected more, his hands moving from the chess pieces to the inside of the robe falling open over my breasts, but there I stopped them. I was a slow starter – nineteen and still a virgin. It wasn't until a few weeks and many chess games later that he finally toppled the queen.

After his checkmate turned me into his bed mate, I stayed at his place almost every night. He read lines with me for the tragedies we sang and starred in as star-crossed lovers on the college stage, from lovers in warring gangs in *West Side Story*, to lovers separated by centuries in *Brigadoon*.

Richard also guided me through the ins and outs, circles and cycles of making love. I don't know who or what banged the walls more, his headboard or the annoyed neighbors.

I opened my mouth in surprise at each new sexual position. I was truly naïve, and he was truly experienced or maybe just well-read in the *Playboy* magazines spilling out of the bathroom rack.

"Why do you need these magazines with me here?" I wondered, appalled at their growing number. "None of those girls could ever love you like I do."

"Doll, you are my living doll. The magazines are just a guy thing, they mean nothing, just a little entertainment and some great articles." So I sneaked a peak at the advice columns, looking for tricks I didn't know, as I carried them one by one, day after day, to the trash chute.

I was entranced by Richard and he showed his love for me in so many ways that I had no doubt he felt the same about me. Still, something gnawed at me deep inside. I never slept well. I started having nightmares, serving up the same recurring theme of bombs exploding.

"You're just describing our love-making," he teased, "or maybe my snores." I laughed but wondered if they meant something more. I wanted to sign up for that "Dream Analysis" class in the Psych department, but somehow never had the time.

One evening when I went back to the dorm to wash my clothes and get some much-needed REMs, I walked in on my five roommates watching a sitcom. Their laughter caught in their throats, as they voiced their disgust.

"Don't you know Richard's the biggest drug dealer on campus?"

"He's been with every girl in the drama department."

"I could swear he was drunk on stage opening night."

"Have you heard of the river Da Nile?"

Oh come on, we all drink, try drugs and sow some wild oats in college. What was this, a planned intervention?

I ignored their jealousy, got my books and clothes, and officially moved in with him. Nothing anyone could say could dissuade me from my knowing that he was the one.

Of course, he'd stop his schoolboy nonsense after school was over...soon. He could stop any time he wanted, and he would want to...for me, right?

~ ~ ~

After tossing our mortar boards in the air, Richard and I were ready to make our mark as actors. I voted for New York and the stage, but Richard (in a deep, Marshall McLuhan-like voice) said, "L.A. is the place, and film is the medium."

So I followed him, full of hope and dreams and everlasting love – right to the Chapel in the Pines.

It wasn't a society wedding, far from it. To avoid the guilt of breaking my Catholic mother's heart, we pulled off Highway 80 in Reno to get married. I had lied to my parents about our living situation at school, but they'd know if we were living in sin now.

His WASP parents didn't seem to care one way or another. In fact, I think they were too busy to give him much notice at all. I had only met them once when they came to our performance of *Brigadoon*. His father explained, "It's a long drive from New York. If he hadn't had to transfer out of Columbia...." Richard always skirted the question of why he "had to" leave there, saying, "Who wouldn't want to live in beautiful New Haven? I'm in the real Ivy league now."

We honeymooned for a day in Lake Tahoe, hiking to a secluded waterfall five miles up a rough, rocky path. We rested on top of a giant boulder to savor the view. Richard took off my hiking boots and gave me a foot and calf rub that moved ever higher, with more and more layers of our damp, dusty clothes dropping off. We consummated our marriage yet again on that rock. But it wasn't as secluded as I thought – when I heard voices in the distance, I tried to cover up, but his hands held me down. I think we got in a few of the tourists' waterfall photos, but Richard didn't care. In fact, I think he was turned on to pose with his bare butt in the air.

"We'll be doing torrid love scenes in front of a movie camera soon, you wait and see," he assured me. "And we won't need body doubles either."

So, did we end up as porn stars or become the serious actors we intended to be?

Well, we did act.

Richard acted as if the modeling jobs he immediately landed were the be all and end all, as they made him the big bucks. I acted as if everything was all right, even though I was crushed, both by casting agents and by Richard's staying out all night partying with other models.

Even though I wanted more of Richard's attention and felt I looked as good as the models, just with a few more curves, I couldn't follow his lead. I didn't want to buy into the bulimia, the diet *du jour* all the other models swore by, so I stuck to acting classes and auditioning for every open casting call.

After a few months, my bikini was hugging me a lot tighter than Richard was, and the four walls of our Tinseltown bungalow started closing in on me in every scene of my *Home Alone* script. I gave in and asked him to introduce me at his modeling agency. He only agreed after I told him, "I'm heading back East otherwise." So, he introduced me to his agent. But I was at least two pounds too heavy for the runway and, who knew, "Beautiful, but not the right type for commercials."

"Honey, you have great legs and lips to die for, but you're too exotic looking. What are you, Mexican, Polynesian, Indian?" asked Agnes. "Our clients are looking for Barbie, not Pocahontas."

I wanted to slap the smirk off her face. My grandfather (the one I had never even met, but whose almond-shaped eyes and pitch black hair I had inherited) was from Madras, capital city of Tamil Nadu off the Bay of Bengal, not Cheyenne, Wyoming!

Still, it looked like I would have to give up the fantasy of being in or on film, and find a real job or, as it turned out, my real self....

~   ~   ~

I got a front-desk job at a fitness club, where they said they appreciated my healthy glow. The flex hours allowed me to continue to audition, and I enjoyed the free aerobics and yoga classes that came as a perk.

I tumbled head over heels for yoga, much like I had fallen in love with Richard – there was no question, it swam in my 1/4-Hindu blood. So what if my parents had brought me up Catholic and the priests and nuns had never mentioned karma or chakras?

I felt like a klutz trying the balance postures and twisted my back out of whack doing a simple shoulder stand, but the chakra meditations played during Savasana relaxation spoke straight to my soul.

"Breathe into the safety and security of the color red as Mother Earth supports you and breathes stability into your Root Chakra. Now inhale the passion of the color orange and feel the sparks of creativity and sensuality light up your Sacral Chakra...."

They were my conversations with the cosmic Dear Abby. Like Carrie's column in *Sex and the City*, dialogues on the spectrum of chakra emotions brought me answers to questions that I didn't even know I needed to ask.

I loved the rainbow of colors associated with the energy centers. My pot of gold at the end of the rainbow of chakra activation, from red at the Root Chakra to violet at the Crown Chakra, was a whole new world – a greater awareness of energy.

Doing the chakra meditations at the end of the yoga classes, I realized that energy was stuck at my Root Chakra, like I was stuck in depression. I had forgotten who I was and then, worse still, I had forgotten that I had forgotten. I was a good person, I really was, but Richard brought out the worst in me and I didn't want to admit it.

My relationship problems with Richard, who stayed home some nights, came and went other nights, never even called other nights, were making me feel insecure and shaky for the first time in my life.

If I asked where he'd been, he'd sneer, "Who are you, my mother?" Then, he'd hug me, apologize and say some version of, "I have to make contacts. The big wigs all hang with the models. But you know it's you I love, just like you love, love, love me, don't you, admit it," he'd say, tickling my anger away.

If I asked if he was drinking (I could smell he was drinking, duh!) or doing drugs, he'd deny it, then stumble to our bed pulling me along with him.

I didn't really know what to make of this new Richard. He wasn't the same person I had married just a year-and-a-half before. He really wasn't. And I had hitched my wagon to this changeling.

Instead of blaming Richard for working too hard in front

of the umbrella lights and paparazzi bulbs, I blamed myself for being less interesting, beautiful and svelte than the models. I fasted on cottage cheese and cantaloupe, but my flattening stomach still didn't entice Richard's full attention.

I was so lonely I began talking to myself in two voices at home. My family and friends were so far away; I felt adrift, my sails ripped, my mast splintered, utterly blown to the winds.

I finally asked the yoga teacher at the club for help. She showed me yoga poses to strengthen my Root Chakra, and gave me a Chakra Handbook that started me on my healing journey.

I was right, I needed to start with my Root Chakra, the seat of our safety and security in the world, the very foundation of our being and our identity.

When the Root Chakra is unbalanced, we may feel fear, anxiety, insecurity, and low self-esteem, I read as the book opened to just the right page.

My teacher showed me some yoga poses, explaining, "Pelvic Rotations and the Butterfly will help increase circulation and energy in the lower abdomen and energize your Root Chakra."

I did them every morning and finished with a meditation where I visualized a red whirling ball of energy in my Root Chakra. My feeling of safety increased until those late evenings when Richard still wasn't home, and dizziness and insecurity rained back down on me.

"I am healthy, happy, safe and secure," I recited over and over. Sometimes, thinking of Richard and his model friends, I changed the affirmation to "I am healthy, happy, safe and thin," until he made it home in the wee hours of the morn.

~   ~   ~

With the holidays arriving and everyone partying, I started making friends with some of the girls at the health club and went with them to see *The Vagina Monologues*. Because the chakras can be the foundation for healing ourselves, for balancing our feminine and masculine selves, I thought they should be given their voice on stage as well.

No one else was writing parts for me, so I decided to pen my own starring vehicle and put my fingers to work for the next year on *The Chakra Monologues*. It took all of my attention when I wasn't working at the club, so I could live in "Da Nile" about my disintegrating marriage.

You Can't Go Home Again

One can never fully "go back home to your family,
back home to your childhood... away from all the strife
and conflict of the world...back home to the old forms and
systems of things which once seemed everlasting but which
are changing all the time."

~ Thomas Wolfe

"Why don't you want to go to my brother's wedding? We haven't been back to the East Coast in over two years. Just think, Christmas in Connecticut," I pleaded again with Richard as we sat in the slow-as-snails freeway traffic.

"Bitch, bitch, bitch. I've told you over and over all week long. I've got too much work lined up to leave at the last minute for a shotgun wedding," Richard said as he pulled into LAX. "Just tell Bill I said, *Congratulations!*"

In the moment before the airport security told Richard to "keep moving along" after he unloaded my bags, I kissed him goodbye and whispered, "If I go alone, I'm staying there."

Not turning to look at his face or wait to hear if he had a nasty retort, I raced through the sliding glass doors and, when they automatically shut behind me, I decided that I had seen the last of L.A. and of Richard and his bulimic bimbos. "I will make my plane, I will make my plane..." I chanted, even as I was slowed down in the security line by a Japanese tour group taking photos of each other walking through the X-ray machine covered in holiday decorations.

Five hours and a plane-load of anguish later, I ran into my brother's arms at JFK's baggage claim. "Wow, three bags, Bec. What are you doing, moving back home?"

"Maybe," I answered.

29

He laughed that laugh we all use when we are not sure if someone is serious or not.

"What do you mean, maybe?"

I was so happy to see him, so relieved to be home, I had tears in my eyes and was all choked up when I admitted, "Oh Billy, the last two years have been hell. Richard's changed. I'm not going back."

"Well, can you keep a lid on the bad news tonight? You're going to ruin my wedding otherwise."

"No worries, I was going to stay through New Year's anyway, so no one will notice when I find a job, and look for an apartment here." I rambled on and on about all the plans I had already scribbled in my new 1999 leather datebook instead of watching the in-flight movie.

My brother pulled off the highway, parked the car in front of a deserted factory in Long Island City (not the best place to linger), and stared at me like I was an alien.

"Stop, Rebecca. Just settle down and let's talk about this."

"There's nothing to talk about. I made a mistake. I thought I knew who Richard was, but he's turned into his own evil twin. I swear."

"Well, tell me all about it. We have a few hours before the rehearsal dinner," he said, pushing his glasses up his nose in the cute way he'd done since he first became nearsighted in grammar school.

"No, you're right, this night is about you, about you and Ellen, not about my bad choices. We'll talk when you get back from your honeymoon...where did you say you were going?"

"Jamaica, mahn, where else this time of year?"

"Well, who gets married in December anyway?" I teased him, punching him in the stomach like old times.

"Well, those lucky enough to be expecting a baby in June, I guess," he said and punched me back.

"Well, double congratulations, Billy, I think it's wonderful. You and Ellen have been together since what, 10th grade? It's about time you proposed, whatever the reason," I said as we got back on the highway into the city. When he helped me out of the car at the Ritz, I hugged him and whispered, "You'll be a great father. And a great husband. Not like some people...."

I followed the bellhop up to my room and collapsed on the bed crying again, happy for Billy, and guilty about the jealousy I felt. It was breaking my heart to go to a wedding when my own heart was aching. I wanted to soak in a bubble bath of misery, then spill my troubles while luxuriating in the arms of family sympathy. Putting on a happy face was going to be hard, but I would try.

After showering and meditating for 10 minutes on my Root Chakra, I felt steady enough to face my parents with a smile. They greeted me in the cold marble lobby of the Ritz Carlton with such open arms, I felt like I was back on our sycamore-lined street in New Haven. "Oh, it's so great to see you, and be here for the wedding, and to be home for Christmas, and to go skiing in Vermont over New Year's..."

"Whoa, sweetheart, we'll be late for the dinner," laughed my Dad, always responsible, always impeccable, always right. "We can plan your visit once this wedding rush is over."

Dad and Mom didn't know my real plans yet, but it didn't matter – I was home, where everyone loved me, just because I was me, not because I was their adoring fan.

"Oh honey," said Mom, so beautiful in her red velvet dress, my own Mother Earth, "why did you stay away so long? And why didn't Richard come?"

"Oh, you know, fame and fortune keep a stranglehold on you."

"Busy toppling Brad and Jennifer from their throne, eh?" she asked.

"Who?" asked my father.

"Ha, ha, ha," was the only response I could think of.

The evening passed by quickly, as I smiled a lot, drank a lot, and lied even more to our family friends about my life in L.A.

The next morning we awoke to a storm that created the most beautiful white wedding day ever seen at St. Patrick's Cathedral. Ellen's father was a good friend of New York City's mayor, who somehow kept the newly fallen snow from turning to mush in the city's gutters until after the limos had pulled up to the hotel for the reception.

The next few weeks rushed by too quickly to actually have the real truth talk with my parents. But I got the promise of an assistant's job from my old drama teacher, checking off at least one of the to-do items peppered across the pages of my datebook.

When I rang in the New Year in front of the blazing fire at the Killington ski lodge with my college gang, they supported my decision to hang around home. In fact, when I told them the truth about my relationship with Richard, no one even looked surprised. Letting it all out was so cathartic that I stopped lying, period. End of story. Which it almost was.

I got back from the ski trip resolved to remain in my girlhood bedroom, a safe cocoon wallpapered with faded rosebuds, but still couldn't find the right words to tell my parents, who steadfastly believed in "to death do us part," that I wasn't going back to Richard.

On the day of my supposed return to L.A., my father came in to wake me before dawn. "Rise and shine, Sleepy Head," he said. "Since you're afraid to fly on those puddle jumpers, like mother like daughter, we have a 3-hour drive to the airport. Mom's already up making your favorite French toast."

"Oh, I can't go back," I said, smelling the warm maple syrup wafts from the kitchen, reminding me of my depleted, starved self in L.A. "It was a big mistake. I want to stay here at home."

"This isn't your home anymore. Your home is with your husband now."

"But, Dad, you don't know."

"I do, I do," he insisted. "I talked to Richard while you were in Vermont and he told me everything. Including the fact that he found producers for your play. He said he wanted to surprise you. I promised him I wouldn't let the cat out of the bag except... You gotta go back, hon."

"But, Dad..."

"Pack up. You've got a husband who's promised to be a man now. The man you thought he was. You got married too young,

Sweetheart, way too young. But it'll work, you'll see. Maybe, if I can talk your mom into getting over her fear of flying, we can even come see you do the Cha Cha on stage."

"Oh, Dad...." I had to laugh. Was I the one who wasn't trying? The familiar feeling of guilt that always tugged at my heart strings compelled me to throw my clothes back in my bags to be tagged for LAX.

Opening Up

"Never apologize for showing feeling. When you do so, you apologize for the truth."

~ Benjamin Disraeli

"**S**o, I came back to L.A. and tried to make a go of my marriage and a go of my play," I said, finishing the long explanation of my "love-at-first-sight fiasco" to the therapist. "But now I have nowhere to go. I'm stuck on your couch, with no desire to go back to Connecticut and face my parents. It was hard enough answering their questions when they were here for the funeral. I have no desire to go anywhere or do anything. I have no husband and no way to forgive myself."

"It's simple...you start by being the person you really want to be, the person who deserves to be forgiven."

Who would that be? What would she look like? I decided to sleep on it for a while. A long while, in between calling for pepperoni pizza deliveries. But I mostly lay awake in my sinking ship of a bed, drowning in guilt and grief. I was afraid to fall asleep. In my nightmares, I saw Richards's blood pooled in the cracks of every sidewalk as his ghostly image followed me like an evil shadow.

~ ~ ~

I hadn't talked to my shrink or anyone for weeks, and got into a pitiful pattern of lying awake at night afraid to shut my eyes, then sleeping away the days to escape my depressed thoughts. But then I was rudely awakened by relentless pounding on my front door. "Yoo hoo," yelled Denise as she pushed open the unlocked door. She followed the trail of music into the dark bedroom where B.B. King was singing "How Blue Can You Get?" over and over and over in time with my deep, dark blue sighs.

"C'mon, rise and shine, it's 4:30 and time for breakfast, lunch or dinner, whatever you choose. I left the set early since you never answer the phone. I'll be in trouble 'cause of you. Now get up!" She opened the curtains to the blindingly bright California day. Then, she kicked away the pizza boxes from the bed, pulled off the covers and grabbed my arm as I squirmed away from this ray of sunshine. "You've got to get up."

I covered my eyes, saying, "I'm not fit for company...."

"You've always been the fittest person I know, and I am not company. Get your yogini-bikini butt up and let's go. That's it, let's go to a class at your gym. You still have your job there, don't you?"

"I never really worked there full-time, just filled in. I called them right after the accident, but I haven't talked to them since..."

"Of course they'll let us in, probably even let us take a class for free. And I'm sure they'll give you your job back. You've got to keep up the rent on this pigsty."

"Oh, I've got enough insurance money to keep me in pizza and a place to live for the next 20 years. With his father being an insurance mogul, Richard had full health, accident, life, or should I call it death, insurance."

"That's good to know. I could use a loan. But honey, please, get up. Remember when you used to tell me to 'leave it at the stage door,' whenever I had problems?"

Okay, maybe I was being overly dramatic, thinking that I had the power to hire a hit man from the universe with my mind. If I was half as psychically powerful as that, then maybe I could manifest peace and happiness too if I put my mind to it.

I slipped out of bed onto the floor where there were some dirty sweats waiting and let Denise pull me up on my feet and out to the Fitness Center where a yoga class was just beginning. Ah, the smell of incense would at least block out the smell of citrus that haunted me at home.

We grabbed some mats and relaxed our bodies for the opening meditation. By the time I was upright in the warrior pose, I felt my blood pulsing through my veins again. In the mirror I saw a smiling face in the back row and at first didn't even realize that it was mine.

Serena, my favorite yoga teacher, came to me after class and after a long, sympathetic hug asked me how I was. When I just shrugged my shoulders and shut my watering eyes, she pulled me into her office where she gave me a brochure for an ashram – right in the Valley. It read: "Come to rediscover your core beliefs and reintroduce yourself to the world."

"It's where I studied," said Serena. "It's a place to find yourself. To move forward."

~   ~   ~

A few weeks later, I found myself telling my life story to a group of intent, open faces sitting in a valley of golden grass and sparkling statues of Hindu gods and goddesses. "So that's why I'd

39

like to study here at the ashram," I explained. "I want to live a better life. I want to devote myself to the path of yoga. I want to change my karma."

"We'll show you the path. How you follow it is up to you. Namaste, welcome," said Gurudev, a tall, darkly handsome Indian gentleman, with a honey-dipped voice and saintly smile.

"Namaste," said the other initiates in just as gentle but weaker voices.

I learned yoga poses to release tension from my body and achieve "union" with the divinity within. I tried to do them just right, but I couldn't mirror the pretzel bodies all around me. I was too stiff. I held on too tightly to find the quiet place inside. It was squeezed out by my ever-chattering, peace-shattering mind.

Would I ever forgive myself? Did I deserve to? Could I spit out the seeds of guilt fermenting in my gut?

Learning from Gurudev that Karma yoga is work or enlightenment gained from selfless action, I thought that might be just the ticket, like the penance I did growing up as a less-than-perfect Catholic schoolgirl. I began working day and night until the kitchen pots were universally shiny, the floors all spic and span. I hoed and weeded the garden and cleaned the rooms to boot-camp standards. While the fumes of Lysol might have scrubbed clean my memories, I was afraid they would also kill some of my brain cells. So I concocted natural cleaners using essential oils, baking soda and vinegar. The kitchen manager tried to get me to use a little lemon too, but I told her I was allergic to citrus. I'm sure she never heard of Calvin Klein's Citrus Spritz and didn't need to.

When I wasn't working, I was refining my yoga poses and meditating, guiltily fidgeting and swatting the flies from my face when no one was looking. I still hadn't found that elusive inner peace, so I listened ever more intently during the philosophy classes.

"Learning to share with complete balance and harmony means we must allow the flow of love and light to fill our vessel first and allow it to be filled to overflowing," Gurudev said. "Then we can easily, effortlessly, and lovingly share it."

One hot day Gurudev sat down next to me where I sat so still, so straight, ignoring the sweat dripping down my spine, staring silently at the inside of my eyelids. He must have thought, "Aha, she has finally gotten it." Yet my mind was racing pell-mell from one disturbing image and thought to another. I opened my eyes when he placed his mocha-skinned hand over my white one. I felt a lightning bolt of energy and knew he had depth and meaning to share with me.

He enticed me, gave me hope, saying, "Let me teach you the spiritual, inward and upward aspect of yoga, of Kundalini rising. Let me teach you to open your heart deeply, increase awareness of the channel of light that connects all the chakras. Let me show you how to connect with higher consciousness through moving your energy upward."

This is what I wanted, the mystical, the miraculous, the unseen energies unveiled. I wanted to learn everything I could about the chakras, their spiritual, energetic and emotional context, not just the dramatic parts we had put on stage.

I prepared for Gurudev's wondrous teachings by moving into an isolated cottage away from the rest of the group for a week-long Silent Retreat. Then on the night of the full moon, he sent me a message to come. My yellow-brick road was lined with golden statues shimmering with life, brilliantly reflecting heaven's moonbeams. Gurudev invited me to enter, to sit down and to join him in breathing. I inhaled deeply into my abdomen, then filled my chest, my heart, then my throat, and my forehead, or Third Eye center with life force. "It is our job to get to the Ajna Chakra, where cosmic energy feeds the entire body," said Gurudev. "From there, with the grace of God, our energy will reach the final step to the Crown Chakra. The Divine is the doer."

That night and for many nights after we spoke little and never touched, but the sparks I had with him were there every time, glowing with electricity.

I would tiptoe into his sacred space for this divine experience, and we would stare into each other's eyes as we breathed into each other's Heart Chakra. I felt a very intense, ecstatic love, for all, for Gurudev.

Gurus hold great power in the eyes of the initiate. I had total reverence for Gurudev, was so thankful for his attention, his teachings, I would have done anything he asked. He was a spiritual master and was opening me to the part of myself I had never really explored, taking me out of my unawakened state and uplifting my consciousness.

One evening he touched me, invited me to touch him, and we engaged in massages that became more and more intimate with the passing nights.

Gurudev taught me the "science of ecstasy," totally and utterly seducing me, body and soul. It was nothing like the only other love-making I had known, with Richard. It was more about connecting to the divine in each other's bodies, holding and moving energy upward without physical orgasm. In its place was a more powerful explosion of energy. I wasn't losing myself, I was finding myself, becoming more and more awake, aware, alive and responsive.

"The greatest source of energy in the universe is sexual," he said, "and sexual intercourse can be a cosmic and divine experience."

So I felt divine night after night, hoping to find my soul, my purpose in life there.

I danced through the heat of the days at the ashram, just waiting for the even greater heat of the nights.

I had grown so much into my love and appreciation for Gurudev that I saw us being together forever. Another fairy tale, I learned, when there was a long, lonely stretch of time when I didn't see much of him at all. I was left alone to meditate on what we had shared. I also remembered Gurudev once expounding on the limits of traditional monogamous sex. I wondered if his mind and body were now cosmically and divinely connecting with new ashram members.

My fragile connection to my own divinity and to his snapped like a thin, dry twig. Giving into doubt and jealousy, I slipped quietly up to his hut one dark, moonless night. Even yards away, I could hear familiar sounds of ecstasy, deep breathing and coupling. I was crushed, whipped around to run downhill to my cottage and ran out of my slipper, cutting and bruising my foot on the steep, roughly-graded slope. Hours later as the sun was peeping over the ridge and I had pounded my feather pillows to pancakes, I had a long self-talk. What had I expected? That Gurudev would be different than every other man? Had my Catholic upbringing left me feeling like I had the right to be both judge and jury?

I wasn't the first initiate Gurudev had bedded and I wouldn't be the last, I learned from the assistant manager, whispering secrets between the tight lips of her Mona Lisa smile. She had probably once been instructed in the tantric arts by him as well.

Okay, I realized, even spiritual leaders are human and could be seduced by their power, as are their students. The ashram was not so different than life on the outside, but...damn him anyway.

What I judged to be Gurudev's lack of pure intentions, true spirituality, as well as my own, overpowered whatever forgiveness I had felt, for others or myself. I knew I wasn't truly in love with Gurudev but had been using him to block out my feelings, my grief over losing Richard, losing my own golden god even before his death.

My heart was still fragile. I once again felt betrayed, less than worthy, destroyed. All the benefits I had felt through the surge of my kundalini opening collapsed. My Sacral Chakra in particular was closed by the bulldozing guilt that overtook me once again. Kundalini cannot rise if all your energy centers aren't open and mine needed constant rebalancing.

I suddenly found it hard to breathe in the dry smoggy air of the ashram. I longed for the ocean, the waves of cool, salty water. I felt dry inside, passionless, devoid of the creativity that had birthed *The Chakra Monologues.*

I made time to concentrate heavily on my second or Sacral Chakra. I knew I needed more emotional stability and confidence in my own sexuality, so I performed special yoga poses like the Camel, the Spinal Flex, and the Eagle.

I meditated on the essence of the Sacral Chakra, flowing water wanting to be moved by the current, not to drown in it. I knew water makes things grow, move, and change and realized that I needed to return to the ocean that I loved.

Open Heart Yoga

"A photographer gets people to pose for him. A yoga instructor gets people to pose for themselves."

~ Terri Guillemets

I moved into Denise's tiny studio in the center of Santa Monica, close to the best natural food stores and restaurants, yoga studios and, most importantly, close to the ocean. She had been a good friend to me during the months of rehearsals for *The Chakra Monologues* and the horrible days after Richard's death, and I looked forward to having her company again. Denise had always been straightforward and honest, on my side when no one else was. But it turned out she and I had little in common anymore, in schedules or activities, and I barely saw her.

Denise had landed a small part in a TV series and was involved with the star of the show. When not at work, they were at the hottest nightclubs or his home in Malibu. She stopped by one evening to change into formal wear and I was excited that he came along and I was finally getting to meet Denise's and the media's darling...until he started dancing around the room taking up all the air in the small space, flirting with me, even giving me a little pinch when Denise went into the kitchen. He didn't seem to care if Denise saw or heard me slap his hand.

Another Richard, another narcissist, I later warned Denise. And she, his willing fan. She assumed I was just jealous. *Déjà vu!*

After that Denise never brought Charlie home again. She only showed up herself once in a while, coming in to change clothes in the wee hours of the morning when I was rising to jog the 18 blocks to the beach.

There Mother Earth called me to kick off my running shoes and dig my toes into the still cool, damp sand as the sun set the dawn on fire. As I stretched, I faced Grandmother Ocean, who answered the questions haunting me, banging around in my head, like whether to risk trying a head stand in the sand and, more importantly, how the rest of my life would unfold, whether I would ever forgive myself.

Facing the ocean, I continued the yoga practice I had begun at the ashram, first concentrating on sun salutations to wake up my body, mind and spirit in concert with the brilliant rays of light filling the sky.

Once I was fully warmed up, I concentrated on chakra healing postures, first to ground my Root Chakra. As I stood in Mountain Pose, then in Tree Pose, I imagined thick roots journeying from my tailbone down into the center of the earth's core, bringing back earth energy to keep me grounded and secure. I saw myself as a palm tree, solid, yet flexing and swaying with the life of leaves and fruit. I breathed deeply, stretching my arms up to the sun, much as a tree does, ever expanding toward the light.

I then strengthened my core with Pelvic Rotations, sitting with my legs crossed at the ankles and my hands resting on my knees as I leaned forward with a so-straight spine. While rotating my torso to the right, I visualized a vortex of red energy spiraling down into the earth. Rotating to the left, I visualized the energy swirling back up into my Root Chakra. Then stretching into Butterfly Pose, I held the soles of my feet together with my interlaced fingers as I fluttered my knees up and down, breath-ing deeply to circulate the healing energy.

Grounded and ready for my Sacral Chakra postures, I stood up into the Eagle Pose, crossing and wrapping my left arm over the other in front of my nose, crossing my left leg over my right thigh, wrapping the left foot around the right ankle. Not as tricky as it sounds. This pose was meant to lock a gentle and peaceful energy into my sexual organs. Bending my knee and straightening my spine, I silently affirmed, "I am able to surren-der my fears. I flow with creative response to what life brings."

I was usually able to stay balanced in this contorted pose for several minutes by focusing my gaze on a stationary piece of driftwood or rock. But one morning a camera flash in my face interrupted my fixed gaze, causing my legs to collapse from under me and a curse (I had tried to give up cursing!) to escape my lips. The photographer who had violated my space, inter-rupted my karmic reverie, offered me a hand up and apologized.

"I'm so sorry. I'm Carter Woods. You were such a gorgeous sight.... I'm taking photos of the 'California Experience,' you know, what tourists can expect when they come here on vaca-tion. The Tourism Association told me to capture the 'beautiful people' doing yoga, surfing, jogging, rollerblading, you know... Your long black hair glistening in the sun, your orange top against the bright blue sky, I had to capture it."

Take that, Dear Agnes of modeling agency fame, I am now posing for a "California Girl" ad!

Flattered to have been noticed by this photographer, rug-gedly handsome with a just-right dimple in his chin and twinkle in his eye, I shook the hand he extended, sorry to see it wore a circle of gold on the ring finger. My Sacral Chakra, the one that had slammed shut with my romantic betrayals, must have opened again. This was the first time since leaving the ashram months before that I could actually feel a spark of attraction toward a man.

If I were to write a book on "How to Find a Guy," instead of sports bars and hardware stores I would definitely recommend Sacral Chakra yoga poses on the beach. A few days after Carter snapped my photo, a man stopped his run on the sand to stand in front of me still breathing heavily as he contorted himself into a mirror image of my Eagle pose, causing me to giggle and lose my balance.

"I'm sorry. I just wanted to join the yoga class," he said. "You looked so serious; it's nice to see your lovely smile."

How could I mind? It felt good to laugh again.

Another morning, a sensuous surprise. A guy actually leaned down and kissed my upside-down mouth as I was bent over backwards in the Camel pose, stretching and stimulating my sacral and heart centers. Granted, my chest was thrust upward and my hips forward in what one might call a "porno" pose, but still.... This was L.A., and I was practically the only female on the beach who didn't have huge boobs with pert nipples busting out of a teeny bikini top in the morning chill. My energized Sacral Chakra must have been sending out a siren call, despite my discreet long-sleeved, high-neck, orange T-shirt and mid-calf yoga pants.

Although I scolded him for his bold kiss, Mr. "Just call me

Jim" sat and watched with rapt attention as I sped through the rest of my poses to end my "show." I accepted his invitation to breakfast at the busy beach café because if I didn't, he said, he would follow me home, and I needed food more than a stalker.

Over mimosas and a heavenly Eggs Benedict, Jim suggested I should teach a sunrise yoga class at the beach. "I'm not ready, I'm just a student. I'm still perfecting my practice," I said.

"Ya know, William Faulkner said, 'All of us fail to match our dreams of perfection. So I rate us on the basis of our splendid failure to do the impossible.' Nobody and everybody is perfect. Life is practice. Perfection is never required, only perfect effort."

I decided then and there to put effort into my love life as well as my yoga practice. I could begin with this kissing philosopher. His bold strokes of self-confidence contrasted seductively with the gentle flourish of his spiritual musings.

I didn't want my love life to end with only two men. I decided Jim didn't have to be my perfect soul mate or guru, but I could trust men again and "enter into the flow of life."

I dated Jim and a few other men I met at yoga classes, coffee shops, health food stores, and walking or doing yoga on the beach. I slept with a few of the few but kept a part of myself withdrawn, pushing them away before they touched my heart too deeply. But I kept looking – at only 27 years old, I knew I couldn't shut the door on love for the rest of my life. So for brief moments in time, I surrendered in the arms of men who made me forget everything, even their names.

One morning I really couldn't remember the name of the guy I was trying to introduce to Denise, who surprisingly showed up for breakfast more and more often.

"I feel like you've turned this place into a brothel," she said to me after he left. "How many guys has it been this month?"

Feeling a little like a slut, I decided to close some of the petals of my Sacral Chakra – perhaps it had opened too far. Oh, there was so much to learn, to find the right balance.

My sexual forays into "like" weren't "love," so I followed others' advice and my own yearning to do what I *did* love. I knew I had to share the knowledge that had sparked me to change my life – YOGA.

I packed my bags and headed to a cliffside retreat center in Santa Barbara to take an advanced yoga teacher's training course. I learned a powerful and dynamic system of Vinyasa Flow Yoga that combines asana (poses), pranayama (breathing) and meditation. With no rulebook or sequence to follow, I felt a lot of room for creativity in flow sequence. And I knew I wanted to devise a Chakra Yoga Flow.

I made a quantum leap in my own yoga practice while seeing how to instruct and set up classes. I learned the purpose of each asana and hands-on corrections to help others perfect their poses or adapt them to their body's injuries or limitations. What I learned, most importantly, was that yoga should never be a competition, but a healing of the body and a stilling of the mind to allow a connection to the divine, or the literal translation of yoga, "union."

With my yoga teacher's certificate clutched firmly in my

hand, I returned to L.A. to find Denise was actually planning to marry narcissistic Charlie and had already given up the lease on the studio. She said she had tried three times to phone and tell me, but they didn't take personal messages.

Okay, I was homeless, so I decided to start driving and stop when it felt right. I found my place farther south in Redondo Beach, near the ocean where I could do sunrise yoga classes, and a community center where I could teach evening classes for those with 9-to-5 jobs. I was determined to make my new career work, if I had to stand on one leg, on my shoulders, on my head, even on my hands.

I put up my colorful flyers for private yoga instruction wherever I could, papering Redondo Beach with rainbows. One morning at the local health food store, as I was sneaking a taste of granola from the bulk bins next to the bulletin board where I was pinning my flyer, I felt a tap, tap, tap on my shoulder. I thought I had been caught red-handed with my fingers in the granola jar. My hand opened wide with guilt and scattered the loot across the worn hardwood floor like I was planting seeds. "I'm happy to pay for this," I said as I quickly turned around to pay the piper.

"I was just going to ask if you had another push pin," laughed Julie, another customer, looking up from the ground where she was now picking up the grungy granola.

She introduced herself as an energy healer and puppeteer who was advertising her "Green Goddess Power" show at Veterans Park.

I had that "I know you" feeling in my gut again. Her warm, somehow familiar smile made me feel happy and snuggly, like

I had just been handed my long lost, forever cherished teddy bear. So I asked if she'd like to have a bite at the deli. Over Avocado Mushroom Tofu Plates, she promised to take one of my yoga classes and I offered to help backstage at her upcoming puppet show.

Whether assisting Julie as she entertained wide-eyed, giggling 5- and 6-year olds, or taking her Reiki class, or entering the surf with her instruction, my whole life seemed better once this beautiful, blonde, angelic woman took me under her wing. Julie was everything I wanted to be – clear, bright, good, kind. I modeled her ways as we spent more and more time together. Yes, this once-cowardly lion decided she, like Julie, could become a healer too.

I took a course in Holistic Counseling so I could add that to my yoga and meditation instruction and maybe mend my own battered and bruised heart. In addition to counseling my own clients, I volunteered at a South Central L.A. homeless shelter.

At first it was hard for me to be strong amidst those who had been swept into the gutter, many giving up on being part of life again. (I remembered the days when I had given up on getting up too.) But these people were both hurting and hungry, cold and wet. When I learned there were over 70,000 homeless people living in the Los Angeles area, I decided to donate not only my time, but my "blood money" as I called my insurance payout after Richard's death to the homeless shelter. I needed to not only help others, but help myself by proving I could stand on my own two feet now.

The resiliency of the kids at the shelter inspired me and

brightened my days. Carrying my brightly-colored yoga mats with me to the shelter, I attracted their attention and began teaching Child's Pose to children who had never had a place to rest.

~   ~   ~

Redondo Beach, November 2004

Days, weeks, months and years had passed and my confidence as a teacher grew along with my following. I set up my own studio, Open Heart Yoga, leasing a beautiful, airy space and painting it with heart-shaped rainbow swirls and chakra symbols.

Opening night was a huge success with all of my clients and all of the neighborhood joining in Dance Yoga under soft pink light as we moved to Aryeh David's "Love's Whispers" CD. My smile stretched across my face like the Cheshire Cat as I watched my parents doing their version of Dance Yoga, the Cha Cha, in the middle of the room.

Even some Hollywood celebs (invited by Denise) made the party. That's right, life had flip-flopped again, and now Denise was staying with me. Having a "girl's getaway," a "reality check," she called it, after she rocketed into stardom via a lead role in an outer-space blockbuster. Charlie, with his fragile actor's ego, or needy narcissism as I called it, became violent when Denise stopped being the constant, unconditional fan, and slapped her one too many times. Even with the restraining order, she didn't feel safe in Malibu, so she moved south to hide out with me, leaving no forwarding address, mellowing out with mantras at the beach, healing under my Reiki hands.

Coked-up Charlie made my ex-husband Richard look like an amateur at doing drugs and other women. From an energy standpoint though, the similarities were too clear when Denise ranted and raved about Charlie's misadventures – they both needed to have the sun shine on them at all times, they had to have adoration or they would stop breathing as surely as they would "Jones" when their bodies demanded another high. I think their over-active Solar Plexus Chakras blocked energy from moving up to their Heart Chakras. Acting with stone hearts instead of loving kindness, they lashed out with jealousy and meanness.

Denise's story wrenched open a Pandora's Box of my own miserable memories of marriage. My nightmares returned, leaving me sweaty and scared. I swam in a slurry of guilt that stained my soul no matter what, no matter how many people I tried to help...my clients, the homeless, Denise.

Following her celebrity friends to my first-night celebration at Open Heart Yoga, the paparazzi spotted Denise with their sharp eyes and long lenses, and her hideout was splashed across the tabloids. It must have helped my classes, because they filled easily. Some star-chasers and paparazzi joined my class hoping to get a glimpse of Denise. They were disappointed that Denise had moved on to a more secluded spot, but a few stayed, enjoyed focusing within themselves for a change, and became regulars.

The stress of starting and keeping the new business afloat without a sound night's sleep left me a little off-kilter though.

To take some of the pressure off of me, and to offer a variety of yoga styles, I invited other teachers to join me at Open Heart Yoga, and they filled the hours of our schedule with Ashtanga, Bikram, Iyengar and other yoga classes. I could focus on what I really loved teaching, Chakra Yoga, both in the studio and, of course, sunrise at the beach. I was still trying to balance my own life, and you teach what you need to learn. "Balance your chakras, balance your life," was my mission statement.

After one particularly long day teaching after a restless night of no sleep, when embarrassingly, I just talked my students through the more difficult balancing postures rather than demonstrating them, I met Julie at the beach. Even a dive in the cool surf hadn't lifted my droopy eyelids, so she said, "You have to get to the bottom of these nightmares. Have you tried Past Life Therapy? Maybe Richard killed you in a past life, and he deserved to die this time around. Certainly from what you've told me and from the tabloid news, Charlie deserves to."

"That's the first time I've ever heard you being so judgmental."

"Well, I'm not big on cheating husbands either. You see, my own father...."

"You never told me."

"It doesn't matter anymore. I'm not the one having nightmares, you are. It's time to see why you can't release evil Richard. I'm serious about the Past Life Therapy."

"Oh, sure. Maybe he was Hitler and I was Eva Braun."

"Seriously, I know a fabulous Past Life Therapist."

"Really? What did you find out about your own past lives?" I asked.

"Well, I usually end up dying a ghastly death," she grimaced, "before I fulfill my purpose as a healer. In Africa I was a medicine man who was trying to warn his people of an attacking tribe when a spear split my chest wide open."

"What???"

"It seems I never survive to fulfill my purpose. That's why I have to keep coming back. Anyway, I got insights into why I repeat negative patterns over and over," said Julie. "I haven't learned the lessons I need to learn yet. But I plan to get it right this go-round."

"It's that simple?"

"Well, I didn't say it was simple, but I'm planning on doing it," she said, looking off toward the horizon, the steel in her eyes not only showing her resolve, but also matching the exact color of the water.

Trouble in the Water

*"I am not afraid of storms for I am learning
how to sail my ship."*

~ Louisa May Alcott

I gasped for air as my head finally surfaced above the unforgiving wave. I had violated the cardinal rule – never, ever turn your back on the ocean. Not even when you're frantically watching for your best friend's head to surface near her board.

After the stars in front of my eyes cleared, I saw she was already on shore.

"Are you hurt?" I coughed up a gallon of sea water as I collapsed on the sandy slope next to her.

"Just wrung out like a rag doll in the spin cycle," laughed Julie, as she struggled to sit up. She intently rubbed her leg through the new zigzag tear in her wetsuit, although she swore on Poseidon's honor that she was fine.

"Maybe we better head off and leave these pipelines to the sharks today," I said as the wind picked up and blew ominous dark clouds our way.

"No – I want to catch one more set. Would you just massage my leg a bit first?"

"Sure, I've been wanting to show off the skills I learned in your massage class," I said.

Anything to take a break from our surfing afternoon...a bit too rough out there.

When Julie gamely said she was ready to go back in, I stalled again – yes, I wanted to tell her about my health problem, but I also saw danger yawing in the jaws of the blue-gray waves.

"Julie, maybe this is a weird time to ask, but do you think macrobiotics could help me with this ovarian cyst my gynecologist wants to remove?"

"Of course, of course, of course," she jumped up for joy, then just crashed back down as her leg went out from under her.

"Well, you don't have to dance like a delighted dervish because I have a 3-centimeter cyst in my left ovary!"

Julie leaned over and hugged me. "Sometimes these things are a wake-up call. You're out of balance, for all your colorful chakra meditations and one-legged Eagle poses. Don't worry about it. I know the macrobiotic cleansing diet can help."

I wanted to change my diet as much as I wanted to walk naked down Ventura Boulevard or spend another hour in the rising surf. Instead of crying, I laid face down and actually took a grimacing bite out of my sandy blanket.

"I'm just so happy you're finally going to try macrobiotics after all these years of me inviting you to my classes," said Julie, as she rubbed my back. "I have a cooking class tomorrow, you know."

"I know, I know," I spat out with a mouthful of sand. "And you know I teach yoga on Thursday afternoons. Can't you just give me a private counseling session?"

"Yes, but it's better to learn how to cook the food and have the love and support of a group. Plus, speaking of love, I want you to meet this fabulous guy who's started the class. I think I'm in love with the way he caresses the carrots while he chops them," said Julie.

"Excuse me here. What else has he been caressing?"

"C'mon. You know I would never...You know it's unethical to sleep with students. I'm waiting until the class is over to invite him over for dinner. There are so few guys who are into a healthy diet. Anyway, once class is over, we'll be on an even footing if, or when, I start flirting," she smiled.

"This guy won't know what hit him."

"Oh, I think he sees it coming," said Julie. "He's got psychic powers or something. Seems to know everything that's coming. Before I even explain a recipe, he starts chopping."

"Psychic powers for sure. Maybe he read your menu and is an impatient know-it-all who does what he thinks comes next."

Looking out at the waves that had thrown her into the rocks below the churning foam, Julie wondered aloud, "He asked me last week how my leg was. I didn't even hurt it until today. Isn't that weird?"

The wind really picked up then, whistling like a horror movie sound effect.

"Well, that proves it. I throw in my towel," I said as I released the rainbow-striped terry cloth into the air. The Santa Anas blew it right back, covering us both in glittering sand. "Okay," I coughed, "I'll test his Third Eye Chakra for special psychic abilities if you'll bring him to my next class."

"No, I don't think he's into that kind of stuff, he just wants to eat better to get rid of his migraines."

"Well, migraines can be related to an imbalanced Third Eye Chakra," I said.

"No, leave it for me to find out," said Julie. "I don't want him to know I was talking about him. He's a little shy. Spends most of his time on a home computer designing video games for Playstation and Xboxes."

"So, what's the name of this introverted carrot character anyway?"

"Mark."

"Probably Millionaire Mark, if his games are any good," I guessed.

"Soon to be my Mark. Hands off, Rebecca. No tossing of that long shiny hair or wiggling of that yoga-toned butt of yours."

"Whatever are you talking about, Prissy?" I said in my best Scarlett O'Hara voice, pinching the leg I had been so nicely massaging. "You know I've sworn off men since..."

"Sure, sure, one creep of an ex-husband and you swear off love forever. Didn't you fall for your guru?" Julie asked.

"That was only spiritual love," I said without hesitation, believing it myself by this time. "The kind I have for you too, or used to," I said, picking up my board and heading for the car, dragging the leash and my sorry love life in the sand behind me.

Yes, most of my time was spent working, teaching, meditating, and surfing, or sharing massages with Julie. Neither of us were dating. I didn't feel I could open my heart to real love again, no matter how many energy healing techniques I had tried. I didn't trust men; I didn't trust myself.

"C'mon," I called back, "let's go. We should stop at the co-op and pick up some Arnica cream to massage into your leg."

Julie looked like a bedraggled sea goddess, limping along behind me, her shaggy blonde hair tangled with curls of brown and green seaweed. She was hurt worse than I thought. Worse than I could ever have imagined.

Macrobiotics Hits the Mark

"Forget not that I shall come back to you..."

~ Kahlil Gibran

Eager or maybe not so eager to enter the world of miso, brown rice, kale and carrots, I arrived at the Macro Center a few minutes past five, still in my sweaty spandex yoga top and tights. Not early enough for Julie's lecture, but just in time to help prepare that night's vegan fare.

I didn't see Julie, only seven women and one man, more appropriately dressed in comfy cotton garments, intently chopping and dicing. I guessed that the tall, dark and handsome guy in the front row was Julie's love interest, Mark.

There was an empty table in back, so I claimed it as my own, wrapped one of the aprons with the big black and white yin/yang logo round my bare midriff, picked up a knife and imitated the motions of the woman in front of me. Just like I had done in my beginning yoga classes. Watch, but stay in the back until you know what you're doing.

"Come here often?" grinned a man who just arrived, even later than me, then picked up the knife at the station to my right.

I jumped, holding up my own knife as if to defend myself.

"Whoa, hon," he said softly, "this is the Macrobiotics Class, not self-defense. I was just trying to be friendly. You okay?"

I had a full-blown case of chicken skin and my Heart Chakra was whirling into space.

Calm down, calm down, he just LOOKS like Richard.

I took a couple of deep breaths, laid down my knife and started gnawing on one of the uncut carrots on my board.

I swallowed before replying, "I don't want one of my fingers to join this pile of carrot sticks."

"First time for you?" he asked.

Of course, the answer was no. I had seen him before. But not knowing exactly what he was asking or how to answer, I just took another bite of my big fat orange carrot, deep orange, the color of the sacral or sexual chakra, the chakra that was pumping out all this energy as I looked at the strikingly handsome macro guy who, behind the horned rim glasses, could have been my dead husband's thinner, older twin.

"My second week. Watch my technique," he said. "The teacher told me I've got my knife work down already."

"Well, excuse me while I keep my eyes on my own carrot," I answered, as mine slid right across the cutting board.

"Here," he said, coming closer to stand behind me, and slowly, sensuously fold each finger of my left hand into the correct position – placing the knife against my knuckles.

"Then, after your first slice, place the flat side of the carrot down, so it's stable while you cut it into sticks."

"Thanks," I think I said, wondering where the lemony smell was coming from as he laid his hand over mine to guide my slicing. I must have been standing there for 10 minutes under the spell of this clone of my dead husband, when I heard the refrigerator door at the front of the room slam shut and Julie call out,

"Hey, guys, I'd like to introduce you to your new best friend – the burdock root! Yes, this ugly brown root is a fabulous blood cleanser and the first ingredient in our miso soup tonight. Watch this special 'shaving' technique to make thin, almost transparent slices."

As my new friend – the guy, not the burdock – moved to his own cutting board, Julie came back to where we were standing, kissed me on the cheek and asked, "So, you've met Mark?"

"Um, not officially," I said, surprised, disappointed and happy all at once, as we shook orange hands. "I'm Rebecca."

"Yeah, I knew you were you," he smiled.

I blanched liked a stewed burdock root. Julie blinked twice, then said, "Oh, I told Mark my best friend was coming this week." She put her arm around my shoulders and said, "I'm so glad you made it."

With eyes begging for help, for rescue from this dangerous *déjà vu*, I asked Julie, "Can I move up front? I'd like to get a closer look at how you cook the soup."

I followed her to the head of the class and stood next to the guy (not so handsome up close) I had thought was Julie's paramour. I didn't look back at Mark, the man Julie had already staked out for herself but who, I knew, was somehow already connected to me.

~   ~   ~

"Salty, yet sweet at the same time. Yum," I said as I ate my second bite of root vegetable stew.

"Be silent and chew," said Julie, sitting to my right. "At least 50 to 100 chews per bite. It's best not to socialize while eating, just concentrate on mixing your food with all those enzymes in your saliva. That's what kept some people alive in the concentration camps. Don't miss out on the benefits of chewing – don't swallow until your food is completely liquid. 'Drink your food,' said my teacher."

"Another bonus – you'll never need the Heimlich maneuver," quipped Mark, who sat to my left.

I smirked but kept chewing, chewing, chewing for another half hour until the impossibly full plate of root vegetables was finally liquefied and swallowed.

"Sort of like an eating meditation," I said through my tired jaw as I put down my spoon.

"Exactly! I'm surprised it's not part of that healthy yoga lifestyle you learned," said Julie.

"I guess there's always more to learn," I agreed as I looked over the list of suggested whole grains, veggies, beans, seaweeds and condiments allowed on my new diet. "Gosh, when I think of all the dairy food I used to eat...."

"Dairy is the worst, especially for your female organs!" said Julie.

"Hey, let's not get personal here," I said, getting up to carry our plates to the sink.

"It must be hard to socialize with such a strict diet," said a sickly-skinny teenage girl who already seemed more worried about her upcoming prom dinner than washing the dishes I handed her.

Julie silently answered the girl by handing out a list of macrobiotic restaurants in the area. "There are lots more than you probably think," she said. "Plus you can always get a near facsimile of a macro diet at a Japanese restaurant," she said. "Many of them serve brown rice these days."

After we washed up and the Wolfe range was shining stainless again, the group started thinning out. "See you next week," waved Julie as she picked up the leftovers and took them into the walk-in fridge.

As he put the last pot back up on the highest shelf, Mark looked down at me and asked, "Want to try one of the macro restaurants with me on Saturday night?"

Why was he asking me? Hadn't he gotten Julie's signals yet? I was dumbfounded and must have looked it, because he said, "Just dinner. No more, no less. Not a crime."

He read me so well, it was a little spooky. And he was definitely attractive, in Richard's leading-man sort of way. At least I imagined he would be if he took off those thick glasses. Actually, I knew exactly how he looked without his glasses.

Oh yeah, I know you. We belong together. But this time I couldn't trust that feeling....

Besides, Julie slammed the fridge door and was now standing there with hands on hips, just staring at me. She was my best, well really, my only good friend since I'd started on my healing path, and I wasn't going to let some sharp slicer come between us.

"I've gotta run, Julie. Thanks for the great class," I said as I made my way to the door.

As I put my key in my car door, I felt a cold hand on my bare arm and the chicken skin reappeared.

"It may sound like a line, but it's not," Mark said. "When I saw you, it was like *déjà vu*...I saw us eating dinner together."

"Maybe you saw us having dinner after class next week," I said, "You know, when you imagined us eating together."

"Not exactly."

"Sorry, but Julie and I have a date with a past-life therapist on Saturday," I said. "Macrobiotics isn't the only new thing I'm trying these days."

"Hmmm, I thought you resembled the beautiful and alluring Cleopatra."

"Pleeeeease. I'm very late. I'll see you next week," I said as I got in my car and buried my blushing face into the cool leather steering wheel until he walked away.

I wasn't looking for anything but peace and balance in my life right now, plus the shrinking of an ovarian cyst. It was a sign my Sacral Chakra still wasn't in balance. So I didn't need any love complications, not even a dinner date. Besides, this guy Mark gave me the heebee geebees. I felt like I had just seen a ghost. Even with those coke-bottle glasses, he looked just like my dead husband.

Besides, Julie liked Mark. In all the years I'd known her, she had maybe two or three casual boyfriends, that's all. It didn't add up. She was gorgeous, smart, the best person I knew. But she'd had too many troubles. As a teenager she'd lost her mother. Had no relationship with the rest of her family. Had been injured in the Navy. What was she running from, that she joined the Navy, for God's sake? I wasn't sure I even believed in God anymore, not the God I learned about in church, but I couldn't seem to leave Him or Her out of the equation.

It's funny that I should worry about Julie's love life when I had none of my own. The only men I seemed to meet were my students, and I had made a vow not to get involved sexually with clients. I had had my flings during my months living in Santa Monica with Denise. But, since starting my yoga path, I had focused within, meditating, not dating, in my free time.

Bottom line, I couldn't do anything to upset Julie. She was ultra-professional and take-charge in teaching her class, but underneath, she was so vulnerable. Too vulnerable. I wouldn't interfere in any way with her hopes and dreams. If she wanted Mark, she would have him.

Into the Past

"My life often seemed to me like a story that has no beginning and no end. I could well imagine that I might have lived in former centuries...that I had been born again because I had not fulfilled the task given to me."

~ Carl Jung

That Saturday, there was no Ouija board, no crystal ball, just a bearded past-life therapist with a Ph.D., a tweed jacket with suede elbows, a matching suede couch, and a relaxing Steven Halpern CD playing in the background.

"Imagine going down, down, down the beautiful winding staircase," he said, putting me into a state of hypnosis (very, very deep relaxation) where I could remember my past lives. My eyes were closed, but the visions before me looked real as could be.

"Tell me what you see," said the therapist.

Well, I see myself. I'm in a hospital. There's blood everywhere.

There are two men in what look to be World War I soldier's uniforms, and I'm wearing a peaked white nurse's cap perched on my head as if I'm about to take flight.

My hands are shaking badly but I'm re-bandaging the wounded head of one soldier, while another, who looks exactly like him minus the wound, tries to hold him down and keep him still. While helping his twin brother, he's telling me which of London's best restaurants he'll be taking me to when my shift is over.

Another nurse – God, it looks like Julie – comes to relieve me. She smiles and says, "Richard, where have you been? I've missed you." He turns and answers, "Hello, princess," and gives her a kiss right on the mouth.

81

I rush out into the fresh air to escape the smells, the blood, the betrayal of wartime. Someone runs up from behind and grabs my arm – it's Richard, the Casanova, the twin who wasn't wounded.

He says, "Thanks for helping Mark. Whew, what a bugger. Let's go have a stiff drink."

"War or no war, there are still morals. You're obviously seeing Julie. Now, off with you. I'm sure she'd like dinner at the London Inn." I send him back with a fierce push and take off around the corner when I hear a huge explosion. Turning back round the corner, I see the hospital suffer a direct hit and collapse into rubble.

"Oh, my God," I say.

"Oh, my God," echoes a woman right next to me. "The Germans are bombing us."

I sat up and bolted out of my past-life regression, out of the present-day session and out of the room. The therapist came after me. "Wait, wait," he called as I raced for the elevator door.

"I have a strange imagination," I gulped out, slamming the down button over and over, "and I don't want to conjure up any more of that kind of stuff." The doors opened and I got on the elevator, resting my head on the cool metal wall inside.

Julie was waiting for me in the corner coffee bar, the only person in there sipping green tea. She was blowing into the hot cup and the rising steam was frizzing the bangs that hung long, dripping down into her eyes. She looked up at me and smiled. So, those blue eyes of hers had not seen the past life where I had left her to die.

I had deserted her in a past life, because of a little jealousy, for a little fresh air. Of course, the bomb wasn't my fault. Of course, I didn't know she had been in love with the long-ago playboy, Richard, the soldier whose arms I had been ready to embrace.

And my husband Richard's car crash years ago wasn't my fault either, so why all the guilt? Was there more to the scene than I saw there tonight? I hadn't dared stay to find out.

Whatever the answers, yes, no, maybe, I knew in this lifetime there was no way I was going to leave Julie stranded. Or betray her. Or date a guy she was interested in. But why did I keep thinking about Mark?

"Well, what happened? Tell me, tell me," she said.

"I need to order a triple shot latte."

"Wait, Bec, that's not on the macrobiotic diet."

"I think I'll start that diet tomorrow."

I stirred lots of sugar in my latte and then sat down next to Julie, reading the menu aloud of all the delicious drinks we couldn't have on the macrobiotic diet. But, that's not what Julie wanted to hear.

"So can you tell me what came up?"

"Only if I chase this caffeine with some brandy."

"Alcohol's not on the diet either," she reminded me. "What could have been so bad? I told you my past life about the spear running me through, and that wasn't pretty either."

"Better let it rest," I said. "I don't really believe in past lives anyway. My mother always said I had too vivid an imagination."

"I thought she always said you were clumsy too, but look at you now, how you stand on your head in yoga class."

"Well, I've taken a few falls doing that."

We left without discussing my past-life regression. Or whatever it was that happened at the therapist's office. I was going to sleep on it and see if it made any sense in the clear light of day. But nightmares woke me as lightning and thunder danced clumsily, bumping against and rattling the pane of my bedroom window. The bad weather didn't faze me. It was the thought of the people that populated my present and past lives, people I had left to die.

I flipped on the light, dragged myself over to my computer, knowing I wouldn't rest until I looked up World War I bombing in London. I thought it had only happened during WWII. But there it was, "Germany's Gotha G.V. bomber had two Mercedes engines and a wingspan of over 77 feet (23 meters). On June 13, 1917, a fleet of Gotha dropped bombs onto London, followed for the next month by daily raids on the capital city."

Dinner for Three

"Love all, trust a few, do wrong to none."

~ William Shakespeare

S econd class, same as the last. Mark squeezing in next to me at dinner, me moving away.

He even followed me to the ladies' room. When I came out, he said he didn't want to ask for my phone number in front of the others.

"Well, thanks for asking, but..." But what? I had no excuse, so I walked right past him into the classroom again before he had a chance to quiz me.

To escape any threesome in this lifetime, I decided that would be the last group class for me. But I'd stick to macrobiotics – already, I was feeling more balanced, less scattered from all the sugar and caffeine in my old diet.

I'd take the macrobiotic cookbook that Julie sold and learn the recipes at home. I was too drawn to this double of my ex-husband to stop myself otherwise, and he wasn't easily discouraged.

Despite my cautionary maneuvers, he caught me just as I was weaving between the other students, leaving class. He gently cupped my elbow, but I felt struck by a fatal blow when he said, "Can we just talk?"

I almost screamed, "No!" but then decided to be fair to him, to Julie, and to myself. I needed to clear the slate, so we walked over to a bench under the arbor of the large banyan tree.

"What did you learn at your past-life session?" he asked.

"Oh, just that I was in World War 1 and lost someone I

loved," I said, unable to get out the full story. "It was horrible."
I closed my eyes, the horror rekindled, feeling hot tears well up
behind my lids.

Mark leaned forward, gripped my knee and whispered,
"Rebecca, don't you remember? I was there with you."

Another punch in the gut.

"Mark, that's really inappropriate. Go find your own past
lives to play with."

I got up, stomped away without looking back, even though
he had spoken the truth, more than I had been able to. I wondered, what did he know that I didn't want to hear?

~ ~ ~

As the song goes, "Sunrise, sunset, swiftly go the..." months in
this case. Julie came over and had dinner with me at least once
a week to check my progress, and her resolve to heal despite
all odds must have rubbed off on me. Six months after my first
macrobiotic cooking class, I had another ultrasound and the
cyst had disappeared.

"Well, the first sonogram must have been in error..." said
the doctor.

"Maybe the macrobiotic diet did the trick."

He looked at me like I was crazy and said, "Let's just agree
you're one lucky girl." I felt lucky and celebrated with a frozen
yogurt in the biggest cup sold, my first foray back into the world
of dairy in six long, long months. It was so delicious I could have
mooed.

Later that day I met Julie to trade massages and to catch her up on the good news about my now non-existent cyst.

"See, I told you macrobiotics could help you heal. You should join our ongoing support group. Mark's not the only handsome guy in it. There are a couple of others you might like."

"Thanks, but no thanks. My intuition tells me that I need to work more on the source of the stagnation that caused the cyst to appear in the first place, not on the diet, although the detox was great, don't get me wrong."

"So you're not going to keep eating the macrobiotic diet?"

"Well, of course I am, in moderation."

"But you'll come to our winter solstice celebration this weekend? And bring a vegan dish?"

"Wouldn't miss it for all the green tea in China."

All week I tried to think of the tastiest recipe I knew how to make and settled on a pie made of millet crust filled with creamed kabocha squash. That's usually really sweet. But now that I had added a bit of sugar back into my diet, its natural sweetness just didn't seem to cut it, so I topped the orange Sacral Chakra dish with a little maple syrup for good measure. Hopefully Julie wouldn't notice.

But Mark did. "Wow, this is great," he said, taking a second slice. "Is it organic?"

"Well, the squash is. Not sure about the maple syrup though, but don't tell Julie."

He raised his eyebrows, then said, "I wouldn't disillusion Julie. She adores you, you know. Just like I do."

"Don't be a jerk. Julie and I have been best friends forever.

How can you continue to hit on me, if that's what you'd call this?"

"I don't know what happens to me when I see you. I can't help myself. Have you ever felt like you've known someone before? And you can't stop thinking about them?"

I knew exactly what he meant. But I said, "Julie loves you and, believe me, she's the best woman in the world. You should count your lucky stars...."

"I know I'm lucky. She's been a great influence. I haven't had a headache in months. Not since she wrapped my last migraine in a cabbage leaf filled with cold tofu."

"And that cured you of them?"

"Well, either that did or the threat of having to wear that poultice in public again."

I giggled and couldn't pull myself away even though I wanted to. I was thinking of the tofu dripping down his face and actually noticed his dark blue eyes for the first time. His glasses were gone. "So, wearing contacts now?"

"No, I never needed glasses. I wore them to disguise my glass eye. You see, I was in an explosion – a science experiment gone wrong – as a child and was pretty sensitive about being called a Cyclops, until Julie made me believe it isn't noticeable."

"Really, it's not. You look great," I said. Just like Richard. And just like the soldier in my past-life vision.

I turned to walk away, but then Julie appeared.

"Great squash pie."

"Well, I have the best teacher," I said and gave her a big hug. "But I'm off. Another party awaits." I didn't fill her in that this other party was a party of one watching the 1945 classic, *Christmas in Connecticut*, on my 18" TV, alone, alone, alone. I loved how the movie was filled with traditional holiday dishes, sugar-laden concoctions and the love-at-first-sight romance like I had had once, just like Mark described.

After Barbara Stanwyck and Dennis Morgan kissed and lived happily ever after, I turned off the TV and dreamt of my own happy endings. I awoke in the morning and tried to shake away a dream I had of myself and Mark lying on a sandy beach, like in *From Here to Eternity*. Julie had been nowhere in sight, which made the dream more of a nightmare.

Chakras in the Balance

"Make the most of yourself, for that is all there is of you."

~ Ralph Waldo Emerson

I was ready to spread my wings. My soul ached to heal the world, and after studying and using the chakra system in my yoga classes for countless days, years, lifetimes, I felt ready to give a Chakra Balancing Workshop. But truly, I knew the healing had to start with me. Teach what you need to learn, I kept telling myself. I still didn't feel balanced with that gnawing guilt weighing down one side of my seesaw life. To build my confidence as a teacher, I concentrated on yoga poses like the Warrior, the Archer and the Boat Pose to strengthen my Solar Plexus Chakra, and visualized the sun's power flowing into my navel center. My Chakra Handbook explained,

"A balanced Third Chakra is manifested in energy and confidence, the ability to follow through and persevere to reach our goals, and a vitality that all can see. The sun is the source of energy on earth and its bright yellow color is also the color of the Solar Plexus Chakra. An unbalanced Third Chakra may lead to indecisiveness, apathy, poor self-image, physical issues with digestion, and addiction to caffeine or sugar...." (Well, that explains my daily trips to the frozen yogurt shop!)

I definitely felt more confident, confident enough to put up my Chakra Workshop flyers. But I knew that balancing the chakras was an ongoing activity. Everyone needs to learn to keep their energy clear. What joy it would be to teach my truth and have it help others.

95

The only fun I had lately was cooking with Julie once a week when she arrived at my kitchen door bearing sacks of whole grains and veggies for our "Macro Mavens" night. She always took leftovers for Mark, just in case they had a late-night date. "He's so busy with work, I'll probably end up eating this for lunch tomorrow. I barely see him twice a week," she complained. "I'm afraid I'm in love for both of us."

"Well, Julie, that's two more dates a week than I have. I'm going to be concentrating on my Heart Chakra once my workshop is over. It's time to forgive myself for my past failings in the love arena and open my heart again, like you have."

"Ya know, I haven't really had any love failings, *per se*, just parent failings – my mother dying when I was sixteen and my father marrying that witch of a nurse who wouldn't even let me see my Mom during her last days on earth.

"And then my health disintegrating – the Gulf War Syndrome the V.A. didn't believe I had," she said, with a big sigh and a sad grin. "But I'm healthier now."

"Seriously, don't you feel like you could use some chakra work? I would love for you to take my workshop."

"Bec, I'm so busy. And even though I'm not that chemically sensitive anymore, I do have to admit I'm tired. When I'm not teaching classes or entertaining Mark, I'm putting green poultices on my leg."

"It still hurts?"

"Not that much, but would you rub that Arnica cream in again?"

"*Mais oui.*"

"Really, someday I'll do the chakra workshop. It just isn't calling me right now."

"I understand. No explanation necessary."

We hugged, finished our mashed millet and cauliflower with shiitake gravy (tasted just like mashed potatoes), then traded massages.

When she left I felt so much better, so energized, that I started putting the curriculum together for the workshop. I included testing of the chakra using my favorite crystal pendulum, then healing techniques for each chakra, week by week, culminating in seven balanced rainbow energies.

~   ~   ~

What can I say? By all accounts, the participants loved the workshop and promised to bring their friends next time, so I decided to hold one in L.A. every year. And I was already booked to do a condensed 7-day class in Hawaii at a renowned Yoga Retreat Center. While yoga is now mainstream in the west, most people still aren't sure what the heck chakras are, never mind why you would want to balance them.

As living proof of the healing power of chakra balancing, my heart felt more open – open enough to at least be dating again...Steven, a writer for the *L.A. Times* travel section, had interviewed me over a cup of tea about my upcoming retreat in Hawaii and that interview led to dinner at his favorite Indian restaurant and dates almost every night since. In fact, he wanted to come along to the Big Island to see the active volcano and stay for the next workshop at the Center too, one called "The Tantric Rainbow."

This Tantric Rainbow workshop sounded altogether different than my experience with Gurudev. The Hawaii brochure read:

"Rainbow Tantric practice is a powerful way to explore our creative energy potential and expand beyond usual limits to a new level of consciousness. The focus is on deep heart connection, emotional safety and respect, with more emphasis on intimacy than on sexuality."

Wonderful! Aloha, Hawaii, here we come.

Tantric Travels

"If everyone you meet is a mirror reflecting you back to yourself, make sure to find a way to love what you see."

~ Don Miguel Ruiz

"Fabulous workshop, Rebecca. I'm so glad we're doing this trade. My taking your workshop and now you participating in my Rainbow Tantra weekend," bubbled Marta, the nude woman next to me in the lava rock warm pond, brimming with ocean water that was heated by underground volcanic springs. Marta was much more comfortable in her flesh than me, but then, she was leading the Tantric workshop.

I had foolishly packed more clothes than I needed since the pool, spa, and beach in front of the retreat center were clothing-optional. But in my week-long class I encouraged the attendees to wear clothing to match the chakra we were working on that day – red for the Root Chakra, orange for the Sacral, yellow for the Solar Plexus, green for the Heart, and on through the colors of the rainbow. I had bought pareos in each color, brilliant Bali silk sarongs that still held the scent of their incense-infused dyes.

To my delight, my workshop was held in the "Rainbow Room," and I was able to turn on a different colored spotlight when I spoke of each chakra. Not much different than when I was on stage with *The Chakra Monologues*. But this audience was interested, their attention riveted, eager to drink from the fountain of chakra wisdom by asking even more questions. We all celebrated the fascinating changes they were seeing after just a few days.

They took my lead and, after cleaning out the center's gift shop, they too began dressing in the color of the chakra they most wanted to balance, as well as using crystals to calm, move, and enhance their energy.

In contrast to my group's explosions of colorful clothing, Marta's Tantric workshop participants wore nothing but the shine of the coconut oil that they massaged into each other's skin. I felt a little self-conscious at first (thank God for the warm, shadowy room) but soon felt cocooned in a safe place, so I cast aside my inhibitions along with my sarong.

The experience was mind-blowing, as they say in this area where the hippie age has never ended...the exercises to heighten sensory awareness worked so well, I practically vibrated at the touch of Steven's finger tracing the warm oil up my spine, from root to crown.

Steven and I felt so in thrall of the love and joy all around us in the lush tropical paradise that we signed up for the advanced week to come as well. We were so in sync, we took out our credit cards at the exact same moment.

In the advanced Tantric workshop, the massage took a more direct sexual turn to raise kundalini energy. It was an evening class and the dark room was lit with only flickering candlelight. Soft atonal music played as Marta led us each to lie down on our mats. Then she instructed us with 10-minute pauses between sentences:

"Massage your Root Chakra or, more specifically, your genitals. Then, with the other hand, massage your Sacral Chakra, or lower abdomen. While still stimulating the genitals without reaching orgasm, move your other hand up to the Solar Plexus Chakra, massaging the navel area. Then the Heart Chakra, or center of your chest. Now, gently massage your Throat Chakra area with both hands, now that your energy has been brought up to the spiritual gates. Finally, let your hands fall to your sides as you focus your inner vision on the Third Eye Chakra area above the eyebrows, bringing the energy up, up, up, toward new sensations and spiritual expansion. Spend time here in silence, opening to visions and spiritual experiences. Finally, place your attention on the Crown Chakra, visualizing the body dissolving into oneness and light."

The next day we practiced this massage technique on our partners, applying the seven steps with slow and rhythmic stimulation – in time with Marta's instructions – to the other person's chakra centers.

~ ~ ~

Maybe because I still held on to the one woman-one man idea of love that was lodged deep inside of me, I missed this paragraph in the brochure for Marta's "Tantric Bliss to the Max" workshop:

"You will find that the degree of sexual interest at class runs a full spectrum, and for some of us, sexual exploration is a natural consequence of an environment where close, intimate, heart-centered connections are encouraged and supported. If any attendee chooses to engage in sexual activities with one or more of the other participants, we have no rule against this. Neither are many attendees likely to have religious or cultural programming against this."

Sounded cool until I walked in on Steven and another fellow in our room massaging both their inner and outer flutes. Open as I'd like to be, I wasn't open to a threesome, as they suggested, or my man having another lover. I got stuck in feelings of rejection and jealousy once again.

I retreated to the front office and weighed my options. I asked the Universe, "Should I stay or should I go?" There were certainly many other healing workshops and classes I could explore at the Center. And the receptionist said they had a new oceanfront cottage available just for me. The green geckos climbing up the office walls chirped their approval, so I checked out on Steven and into a cottage of my own.

That night at dinner, I sampled the many exotic flavors of the buffet. My fave was the miso-coated mahi with brown rice and macnut pilaf (I couldn't wait to share this recipe with Julie – it was macrobiotic with a tropical twist, perfect for this hot climate). I also studied the large blackboard with the smorgasbord of class options from Kirtan chanting to Emotional Freedom Technique (EFT) and Ecstatic Dance to a Huna Healing Circle and a week-long Hawaii Health Getaway set to start the next day.

After dinner I ran down the plumeria tree-lined path to the office to sign up for a massage. Sherri, a friendly EFT practitioner with doe-like eyes, was putting out flyers when I walked in and I was happy to take one.

"I have a free hour right now if you'd like a complimentary intro," she said.

I was drawn in by her serene smile and the adorable "tapping" teddy bear in her arms and couldn't help but use the cliché, "Looks like I'm in the right place at the right time."

We walked out to the meditation bench on the cliff overlooking the ocean and I had my first experience tapping my stress away as the sun's last rays dropped into the ocean.

Although I've since forgotten the many points on my body she taught me to tap to change my limiting beliefs (like, I'd never have a good relationship), I'll never forget the affirmation said aloud at the start of the tapping sequence -

"I love and accept myself even though..."

Yes, if I could only love and accept myself even though... what a beautiful thought.

Sherri walked me back to my little cedar cottage, which was much cooler, closer to the ocean breezes than the overheated one I had shared with Steven. She left me with a bear hug and told me what to wear for my 8-p.m. Lomi Lomi massage.

I was determined to move on during the week ahead without any tension from my rift with Steven, so I was glad I was working on both my emotions (with EFT) and my body (the Lomi massage). I was told it would pound away any tense muscles.

Aunty Leilani, a walnut-skinned Hawaiian massage therapist with the most beautiful cascade of dark hair, asked me if there were any specific problem spots I wanted to work on. I told her I had a kink in my lower back.

"Well, that's just anger, let's release that."

"Anger," I snapped, "I've released all my anger already."

"Not if you still feel tension. Now, tell me, how can you not be happy and peaceful here?"

"Oh, I'm happy to be here, but your problems travel with you wherever you go. From one life to another. From Connecticut to L.A. From California, which now feels like another world, to Hawaii. Whatever time or place, every relationship in my life gets destroyed."

"We all have baggage that is better left at the airport," said Aunty. "Now, we will perform a Ho'opono'pono to heal your relationships." In ancient Hawaii, she explained, they had a process of talking out conflict, forgiving one other, then letting it go forever. Any mention of past grievances would cause the person to be banished from the village.

Hmm, no wonder I felt banished from my own life.

She chanted in Hawaiian and then danced around the massage table as she massaged soothing aromatic oils into my sunburned body (burned in areas that had never even seen the sun in California). As my muscles released, so did that overruling feeling that I was at fault and to be blamed for everything "negative" that had happened in my life.

Guilt, after all, is just anger turned inward, Aunty explained.

I believed her when she told me, "Everything is Working Out Perfectly, EWOP for short."

The next day, feeling lighter and freer than I had in many a lifetime, I took a morning acro-yoga class. Whether it was due to bravery or recklessness, I found myself swinging upside down on a scarlet silk scarf tied to the branches of a coconut tree towering above the jagged ocean cliffs. I felt a tightening in my gut when I looked down at the rock-filled spray of bright blue waves below and realized that familiar tight feeling of gloom in my gut was just "Plain Jane" fear. Fear of ruining things, fear of being alone, fear of being unlovable or unworthy of love. Fear of falling off a cliff. Just plain old fear. Remember Everything is Working Out Perfectly (even if upside down or backwards, I told myself to increase my POWER).

I'm so glad one of my classmates took a picture of me swinging in the trees or no one at home would ever believe this. When he showed me the photo on his smart phone, I saw a bright yellow aura (or was that the sun?) surrounding my Solar Plexus – what used to be the center of my fear was now the center of my power.

That evening after the acro-yoga group left the center, the glow of swinging freely started to fade. I felt loneliness creeping back in from the dark side, like a pair of night geckoes on my window screen that I named Morose and Melancholy. I was so glad when the rest of the Hawaii Health Getaway group arrived from the airport in time to meet me at dinner.

We introduced ourselves as we picked from a bag of colored crystals – stones in the colors of the rainbow, each one correlated to a different Hawaiian Huna principle.

Without looking, I let my intuition do the choosing. The one that tingled when I touched it turned out to be a green stone, which from the perspective of the chakras, meant I should concentrate on my Heart Chakra (meaning love and forgiveness) during the week.

Kiana, the group leader, said green was also the color of the Huna principle, Aloha, which meant Love. Wow, all ancient wisdom agrees on basic principles. Maybe if I hear the same thing enough times, I'll begin to really get it, I thought.

"The principle of Aloha is translated as: To Love is To Be Happy with...someone or something," Kiana said, "so just focus on what you like and ignore the rest. It's the only way to be happy. There are plenty of things to love here in beautiful Hawaii, so it's a perfect place to practice. Let all blame and criticism just fall away. Praise and bless everything that symbolizes what you'd like more of in your life. And you'll get it."

So this was the perfect place to heal my heart. And my Heart Chakra! I felt that I had been in a never-ending search for true love and compassion, especially toward myself. So, I took out my Chakra Workshop notes about the Heart Chakra. Would I ever read them enough?

"All healers work their magic through the power of love. And we can all heal ourselves – by releasing the tension that stops our healing energy from flowing. How? Through love. Open your heart chakra, and feel the love and compassion flow through yourself and out to the world. Signs of an unbalanced Heart Chakra include anger, depression, despair, jealousy and grief...."

Yes, I was ready to let go of Richard, to let go of Gurudev, of Steven, to scream and shout "Goodbye!" The innocent tourists walking by my cottage turned and waved goodbye to me, and I waved back, using them as symbolic representations of my guilt and grief.

I concentrated on yoga poses to open my Heart Chakra: The Spinal Twist, to open and expand the heart center. Then the Head of the Cow, where you reach your arms – one up, one down, to meet behind you in the middle of your back, opening up the chest and relieving tension in the back and shoulders.

I also learned an exciting, quick-yet-profound energy healing tool from Serge Kahili King, Ph.D., founder of the Huna group, Aloha International. Dynamind seemed like a simpler version of EFT and it did have similarities to it, Dr. King said. "In Huna, we try to make things as simple as possible, as effective as possible, so we've combined the power of words, breath, movement and feeling into one instant healing technique."

Dynamind can be used to heal a wide range of physical dis-ease, he explained. Simply state out loud what you want to change – the problem, pain or discomfort – and by tapping and breathing, you feel the problem (pain or discomfort), and the tension that caused them, fade away.

Dr. King advised asking myself what emotion was a problem and where I felt that emotion in my body. Changing that physical sensation would let the healing energy of the body once again flow freely. "All emotion manifests within the body with some physical feeling," he said. Just as chakra imbalances can manifest in uncomfortable physical and emotional problems.

I found myself thinking of how guilty I always feel and searched my body for a corresponding sensation. When I found it, I repeated my personal problem, "I feel tightness in my back, and that can change. I want that feeling to go away," as I held my hands in a loose prayer position. Then I tapped four spots, the heart center, the web between the thumb and first finger of each hand, and the knob at the back of my neck where it meets the shoulders. I finished with a deep breath, inhaling with my attention at the top of my head and exhaling with my attention at my feet.

Emboldened with my new power to direct my inner, sub-conscious actions, I also tried, "I feel cramping in my stomach from fear and that can change," and "I feel the ache of grief draining my energy and that can change," and jumped with joy at how the stress ebbed away the more I used Dynamind.

Huna wisdom and the aloha of the group made me feel like I had found what I'd been looking for. So I stayed on the Big Island. Many people, I learned, come to Hawaii on vacation and are led to stay, for an extra week, a month or sometimes a life-time. I was one of them. I didn't even go back to California to pack up. After all, now that my hurt and disappointment were no longer part of my baggage, a few pareos and my computer were all I needed. I planned to live at the Retreat Center and to take as many workshops as I could in exchange for giving yoga and meditation classes. Wow, what a life!

Tripping Over the Past

"There are only two mistakes one can make along the road to truth; not going all the way, and not starting."

~ The Buddha

I made lots of new friends. You couldn't help it in the land of aloha. And though I didn't mean to ignore the loved ones I had left behind, I did. I hadn't spoken with Julie in more than six months when she called me, frantic, her voice strained and nearly inaudible. But I understood that she was sick and needed help.

I walked up the hill for better cell phone reception and realized how isolated I had been from the worries of the outside world. But now they were closing in.

"You know that pain I've had in my leg, you know, forever?" she asked.

"Of course I remember. What is it?"

"I have Stage 4 melanoma."

"What???? How many stages are there?"

"Four. It seems I have tumors from my hip to my ankle now."

"Oh my God, Julie, how did the doctors not notice this before?"

"What doctors? I haven't been to a doctor since I was treated so badly at the V.A. hospital. I did show the gynecologist there the mole I had on my hip 10 years ago, but he said it was nothing. So I ignored it until the pain started a couple years ago. Then I used poultices and energy healing to treat myself. The doctor said he was impressed I've lived so long. Can you believe he said that?"

"Crazy. Am I really hearing you right? What is that infernal buzzing? Is Mark with you?"

"Oh, it's the phone I guess. Well, first Mark said he didn't think he was strong enough to see me through this. That I needed a better boyfriend. A real smack in the face."

"I don't believe it. Where are you now? There's so much static on the line."

"We're in Mexico. I decided to try the herbal cancer cure here, and Mark came with me. He stuck by me after all. But the treatments took all my pesos and most of Mark's and now the clinic here has actually given up on me too. They said, 'Adios, your cancer is out of control.'"

I took the next flight out of paradise and moved back into my sublet house, gently showing the beach bum (who had never paid the rent anyway) to the door.

I had learned so many new modalities in the hotbed of Hawaii's alternative health community that I thought I could really help Julie.

I didn't care if the oncologist said she had Stage 4 melanoma, a sure death knell according to all the info I read on the web. I wanted to do another Chakra Workshop in L.A. and have her attend. I knew in my gut it would help her get to the root of her disease...the first step toward healing.

The bells tinkled on the door of the New Age bookstore where I was posting a workshop flyer. I turned around and came face to face with my past lives or, I should say, the Past-Life Therapist. If not his face, now minus the beard, I would have recognized the dusky smell of suede elbows on his tweed jacket anywhere. With a chuckle, he asked, "Aren't you the lead singer of The Runaways?"

"I think you're looking for Joan Jett," I joked back, even though I knew the Universe had sent him looking for me.

"No, I meant my personal runaway."

"Sorry 'bout that. I freaked out a bit."

"A bit."

"I guess I still owe you for the session. Let's see…three years of interest would make that, what?" I asked, counting on my fingers. "I expected you to mail me a bill or something," I apologized.

"I did, but it got returned with no forwarding address. Why don't you come back into the office and explore whatever it was you were running from? Maybe you're still running from it and, believe it or not, that kind of closure would give me more satisfaction than getting your bill paid, and probably do you some good."

I looked this man in the face, really looked at him closely for the first time and saw the great kindness in his smile, the sympathy in his eyes, and heard the promise of closure in his steady voice.

"It's possible to release the karma and the emotion that was created in another time," he assured me. "If you stay long enough I can even teach you tools you can use to see other times and spaces by yourself and go much deeper into yourself. Many times it's the only therapy that helps in healing an emotional or mental, sometimes even a physical, issue."

"You've sold me. I guess I'm brave enough to find out what happened next. It has been haunting me, always in the back of my mind," I admitted for the first time.

"What are you doing now?" he asked. "I'm headed back to my office and don't have another client until five o'clock."

"I guess I'm about to enter Back to the Past, Part II."

"I don't think you're really taking this work seriously."

"Oh, I have to joke about it some, because it scares the hell out of me. You really have no idea how seriously I have been taking the vision I saw in the last regression. I think that scene may hold the key to the feeling of guilt that seems to be the theme of my life."

~   ~   ~

"Okay, now take three slow, deep breaths. You're stepping on an escalator going down, down, down. Go down step 1, 2, 3, 4, 5, 6, 7, 8, 9, 10. You're back in the past life where you were a nurse. There was a bombing. What do you see around you now?"

I'm running toward the hospital where the bomb went off. The wing where I had been just minutes before is bursting with black smoke, but it is still standing. I cover my face with a handkerchief and climb through the soot-covered mortar, splintered wood, twisted gurneys and, oh my God, body parts. The dust of death hangs over everything, and I know I'm staring straight into the maws of hell. I look and look for the people I left behind. I don't see them.

"Keep searching, Rebecca. What do you see?" asked the therapist.

Fire Wardens are blowing whistles to call stretchers over for the wounded. Oh, there's the man Julie was bandaging, the man I assume is Mark. The one with the bloodied face. But I don't see Julie.

"Keep breathing, keep looking Rebecca. What do you see?" asked the therapist.

I'm screaming, "Julie, Julie," until I hear a weak whisper of a voice calling back to me. She's trapped under a fallen beam, and I can't lift it.

The wardens finally come to help, but it's too late. Her eyes are open, but her breath is gone. The beam crushed her chest. I sit there holding her in my arms for minutes, for hours, until the Fire Wardens carry her lifeless body away.

I walk over to Mark's bed and he's actually in the one place left intact, an island in the middle of hell. He's calling for Richard, who is lying on the floor near the now-shattered door, shards of metal and glass marking bloody holes in his uniform. I kneel down next to him and, with his last effort, he lifts his eyes to me and just says, "Mark. Find Mark."

I shook the vision out of my head, stretching upright from my comfortable position on the suede sofa. "This is an awful story, I'm stopping now," I said sadly, still feeling woozy, too scared I'd fall if I stood up.

"What are you afraid of?"

"I rejected Richard, the soldier in my past life, sending him to die just like I did my ex-husband, Richard, in this life. And I let Julie down in that life. If I'm not careful, I might do it again in this one too."

"Why would you think that?" he asked.

"Well, she's sick. Really sick. And I don't know if I can help her. Plus it seems we were attracted to the same man in the past life and in this one. I don't want to be the cause of her losing out this time."

"Well, forewarned is forearmed, they say. Are you both interested in the same man *now*?"

"Oh God, can we save this discussion for another time? I'm really mixed up right now. No, I'm not interested in Mark, her boyfriend. I mean, I would be if she wasn't. Oh, I don't know what I mean. I'm a mess. And it seems like I was in a mess in my last life too."

"How about we schedule again for next week? My 5 o'clock client has been waiting," he said.

Gratefully I wrote him out a check, but he and I both knew I wasn't going to keep my next appointment.

I went directly home and affirmed over and over my intention for the chakra workshop, a quote I had taped on my wall:

"Be a Catalyst for Wholeness. Be a Motivator of Spirit.
Be a Messenger of Love and Light. We all are
Mystics, Prophets, Seers and Sages.
We all have within us the Knowledge of the Ancients
and the Wisdom of the Ancestors. Seek your Authentic Voice
as you Evolve towards Enlightenment. Be a Loving Spiritual
Guide to Everyone you meet.
Plant Seeds of Positive Thought. Plant Seeds of Conscious
Transformation and Plant Seeds of Harmony and Balance.
Be the Master of Miracles you were Born to Be."
~ Michael Teal

Into the Rainbow

"If you want OTHERS to be happy, practice compassion. If YOU want to be happy, practice compassion."

~ The Dalai Lama

That first Wednesday night class, as the sun dipped lower into the pink smog, I strode into the dark community center hoping the bright rainbow colors of the chakras would transform the room like the sweep of a fairy godmother's wand. That it would look as magical as the Rainbow Room in Hawaii. Too bad I had given up the lease on my yoga studio. But I could transform this space. I was sure I could, hanging my favorite multi-faceted crystal in the cleanest west-facing window so the sun would send rainbows of refracted light through the dust motes.

I switched on the overhead lights just as Julie walked in, glowing with sun-kissed skin now darker than her golden blond hair.

A few weeks earlier, when she had called me in Hawaii on a crackling land line from the Mexican clinic, I listened and sympathized to her static-broken sobs, then stubbornly insisted she get a second opinion at L.A.'s most respected oncologist's office. And attend my upcoming chakra workshop.

"What, you're coming back to L.A. to give a workshop? I can't wait to see you – I've missed you so much!"

I had my own ideas about Julie's chakra imbalances, but I wanted to pass the pendulum over her body and let her see for herself where the source of healing might lie. So I had quickly arranged this class and, luckily, seven other people signed up.

Always the caregiver, Julie told me to relax and organize

my handouts while she lit the beeswax candles in their stained-glass holders and turned on my favorite CD of angelic music to welcome and relax the group. The swirling harmonics of harp, flute, chime and singing bowl tones soothed the clanking squeals of the metal chairs as we folded and closeted them. Julie then arranged my soft, silky mats in a perfect circle of color, before collapsing right down in the middle of the rainbow, on the bright green one.

I turned off the blaring overhead fluorescents and aimed a mini-spotlight toward my favorite chakra poster resting on the easel. It would help keep our focus and help me to explain why the chakras are so important to our health....

"Chakras are the vital energy centers within the body," I told the five women and two men who had joined Julie on the cushions. "The lower three chakras cover basic life necessities: security, sexuality and self-esteem. The fourth or Heart Chakra deals with love and compassion and is the bridge to the upper chakras, which are associated with communication, intuition, and connection to spirit."

"Why are they in the colors of the rainbow?" asked one woman trying to sit comfortably on the floor in a tight business suit.

"Chakras appear like seven spinning wheels of light," I explained, "each emitting a different light frequency, which is seen as a different color, starting with red at the Root Chakra up to violet at the Crown Chakra."

"Is there scientific proof of them?" asked another voice.

"Well, since ancient times, mystics and healers from India

and Egypt to South America depicted the chakras as light emitting from the physical body. In recent years, Kirlian photography of the body's aura and electromagnetic measurements have confirmed their existence."

A few of my students started squirming and readjusting their mats, so I stopped with the technical and returned to the realm of hope, promising, "When you learn how to balance your chakras, you'll see changes in your health and energy and perhaps even change the course of your life."

"Money-back guarantee?" Julie asked in a whisper.

"Would you like to go first?" I asked as I took out my crystal pendulum. Julie formally bowed to the group, got a chuckle, and then laid down very ceremoniously in front of me. I swung the crystal pendulum over each of her chakras.* It swung clockwise (showing the chakra was open and balanced) on her lower three chakras, counter-clockwise (showing a closed chakra) over her heart, and hung still over the upper three chakras (showing blocked energy). Tears dripped down her cheeks.

"Julie, this isn't a pass-fail test, just an indication where healing can start," I tried to soothe her as the next person lay under my pendulum.

~   ~   ~

I followed Julie back to her condo after the class. She was so upset.

*Order your own crystal pendulum for chakra testing at www.TheChakras.org.

"I've done nothing but practice forgiveness, I swear. But how does it really work? When your father is a bastard? When the Navy tells you you're crazy after they deliberately expose you to chemicals?"

"I've found it hard to forgive too, especially myself. But I've learned so many new tools in Hawaii."

"Shall I get out the tennis rackets so we can slam the feather pillows?" asked Julie.

"First, let's make the decision that whatever happened in the past no longer has to affect us now, deal? That doesn't mean we have to condone anything, it just means we're not going to let it stress us out. It only hurts us, and no one else, to hold onto anger."

"Deal," agreed Julie. "But exactly how do we do it?"

"Well, I learned an energy clearing technique called Dynamind from Serge Kahili King, a shaman in Hawaii.

"When you think of your anger, where do you feel it in your body?" I asked.

"In my chest, it's really tight, and I have a hard time taking a deep breath, just like when I was in Iraq and the bombs were exploding. It's like a heavy weight on my chest."

Rubbing my red, burning eyes, I still saw the vision of Julie in my past-life regression.

I led her in tapping away the tightness in her chest. Then we brought in healing green light with a chakra meditation:

"To send forgiveness, wrap those people who have caused you pain in bright green light, cleansing and healing the situation. Release yourself and them from any negative connections,

only keeping the good. Let go of anger to have space for love to grow. Now, with love and compassion, envelop yourself and your whole life experience in healing green light."

After a few minutes, Julie opened her eyes, which once again were brimming over with tears that left sad trails on her sunken brown cheeks.

"Julie, what do you feel?"

"I do feel lighter and I do feel love and forgiveness. When you're faced with life and death, nothing seems so terrible anymore. I forgive everyone who's hurt me in my life. I do. I do, I do. But some hurts, like my chemical exposures in the military, may have damaged my cells beyond repair, even beyond the hope of a miracle.

"When the oncologist gave me the results of my biopsy, you had to see his face. He couldn't hide it. He knew I'm a goner. And the specialist you found for me...well, all he could offer was a chemo trial for Stage 4 Melanoma patients using strong new drugs that may kill me before the cancer can. I'm going to be a guinea pig for new chemo cocktails. They don't even pretend that I might be cured."

I put my arms around Julie and cried along with her. Were miracles possible? Please, for Julie, please.

Mark in the Spotlight

"The truth needs so little rehearsal."

~ Barbara Kingsolver

The fifth week of the workshop, Julie called me and said, "I'm puking my brains out here from the chemo. Can I send Mark in my place to your workshop tonight?"

"Don't you need someone there with you?"

"No, I'd rather be alone right now. And Mark's losing it. I'd like him to focus on just himself for a few hours. Try to help him too, okay?"

"Of course, you know I'll do anything I can."

So Mark joined the Chakra Workshop that night in Julie's stead. He sat in our circle, and followed along with the exercises to balance the Throat Chakra.

"Now that you've learned to balance your four lower chakras," I said to the group, hoping Mark had followed along with Julie at home, "you have balanced the energies necessary to be grounded in the physical realm – security, sexuality, identity and intimacy. The fifth chakra, the Throat Chakra, is associated with expressing your truth to the world. Balancing this chakra will help you communicate your feelings, speak honestly, express your inner truth, and receive and process information from others.

"Do you have any of these signs of an unbalanced Throat Chakra? Shyness, criticism, excessive talking or an inability to verbalize your feelings, chronic sore throats, TMJ or stiff necks, or an addiction to smoking?"

A few nodded their heads, so we took out our mats to do some yoga poses to balance this chakra. I led the group:

"Start with Chin Press Breath, affirming, 'I am able to hear the voice of my soul.' Now, loosen your neck and shoulders with shoulder shrugs and circles. Good, breathe with it. Now, let's do the Fish pose followed by the Half Shoulder Stand."

Down to our mats, the group relaxed into corpse pose for the Throat Chakra Meditation:

"Breathe in sky blue light, then fill your lungs and open your throat wide as you sing whatever tone or note feels right!"

The room echoed with joyous noise.

~   ~   ~

Before we closed for the evening, during our sharing time, one of the students, Jean, talked about how tired she felt...always. Mark suddenly jumped to his feet and yelled, "There's a spirit sapping your strength."

"What?????" Jean screamed.

Most of the room turned to Mark, looking at him like he was from Mars.

"Yes," Mark explained, "maybe because we've been working on the Throat Chakra tonight, I was able to speak out about it. I've always been able to see spirits, or maybe sense them is the better way to put it, but I usually keep it to myself. I'm sorry if I frightened you."

"No," said Jean, "You may be right. I've always known my grandmother's spirit jumped into me when she died. But when

I mention it, people think I'm nuts. So I keep things to myself too."

"What a revelation, Jean," I said. "Let's do some exercises to strengthen the Solar Plexus Chakra, with the intention of casting off any outside energies that may be hanging in any of our energetic fields."

Suddenly, this new guy, this stand-in, Mark, became the most popular person in the group. After class he was surrounded by the other seven students, all wanting a psychic reading. But he refused, saying he didn't really know how to do that.

"I shouldn't have blurted that out to Jean," I heard him explain, "I'm not a trained psychic, I just sometimes see or hear things."

The disappointed group eventually wandered off, although Mark ostensibly stayed to help me straighten up the room. But I felt he wanted to explain himself without an audience. I was piling up the silk Indian mats and was about to blow out the candles when I saw him just standing there, tears dripping down his cheek.

"I'm so afraid," he said. "I feel helpless. I warned Julie that I wouldn't be the best person to see her through all this. But she wanted me to stay with her. I've tried to be strong. I just don't know how to..."

"Mark, you've given Julie the greatest gift possible – you're there for her. You love her. You stayed with her, when a weaker man would have left. What more can a person give?"

"But I can't handle this feeling that I've already lost her. I don't know what to say to comfort her. I'm more comfortable playing out my feelings, my talents, my visions, with strokes of computer keys and binary code. I stare down the apocalyptic demons in my video games, but yet I can't look Julie in the face anymore."

"Yes, you can. Look her right in the eye and breathe with her – from your heart to hers and back," I said. "Believe me, it will bring up all the love, compassion and forgiveness you need."

"You're psychic too. How did you know I needed forgiveness? I think I'm angry at Julie for leaving me, as if she got sick on purpose. Or maybe I'm mad at myself. It should have been me fighting in Iraq and defeating cancer, not her. But this beautiful, fragile woman is the warrior. While I've always been different."

"What do you mean, different?"

"No other kid in the neighborhood had an eye blown out in a science experiment gone awry. I shouldn't have been sitting on the table where my brother was mixing his new chemicals. The explosion was the last thing I saw with two good eyes. I wouldn't still be blaming him except that he led the gang of neighborhood bullies who taunted me, nicknaming me 'Cyclops.' He used to steal my glass eye from my bedside whenever he woke up before me. Once I found it floating next to the blueberries in my bowl of Rice Chex. Go ahead, laugh. Even my mother did."

His Throat Chakra was wide open, he was on a roll, so I just smiled and nodded in sympathy.

"Then I went through puberty, and I got blinded again, this time by the rush of hormones that lit me up with migraine auras," Mark said. "When I got one of those headaches, I saw lightning flashes whether my good eye was open or closed. The pain, the thunder that always followed the flashes, would drive me to my knees, but I never explained to the other kids. They already knew I was different."

I stroked his arm, trying not to stare at his eye, but he caught me looking.

"It's okay, I'm used to it now. And then I always visualized the little bastards when I shot, kicked or exploded the enemy in my video games. The doctor had told me when I was a teenager that the migraine auras and headaches would go away when I got older, but he was wrong. They didn't go away until I met Julie and learned her healing ways.

"Julie didn't seem fazed a bit by my poor track record in love, my lack of a right eye, or even my migraine attacks. She gave me countless massages and Reiki sessions and served me savory macro stews – until my light sensitivity was gone. She took me out of my chattering mind and into the clear channel of my heart. My visions, my dreams of real life came into focus as clearly as if I had a hundred eyes. But now she's fading away."

My heart was breaking over Julie too. I felt an avalanche of lost hope crashing down on those of us foolish enough to defy the warning signs to "Give up and move on, Julie is gone."

I paused from my own sorrow to offer Mark what little help I could – a journal.

"Take this chakra diary and write your story down. Believe me, it will help. Bring it next week, along with Julie; God, I hope she's well enough to continue with the workshop. Tell her, if she'd rather, I can come over to visit her."

The Point of No Return

"Love is, above all, the gift of oneself."

~ Jean Anouilh

I called Julie every day to check in and went to visit as often as I could. But yesterday, when I called, she didn't even recognize my voice at first when she answered. I had obviously woken her up.

"Please just wait for updates from Mark, okay? I'm sleeping at odd hours now and I have no good news to give you. So I'd rather Mark just email my friends with updates."

Even though I knew it wasn't intended that way, I felt rejected by the one person I had loved unconditionally in this lifetime, in all of my lifetimes.

"Of course, whatever you want. I'll check in with Mark," I said. "Is he coming to the chakra workshop tonight?"

"I'm sure he will. I want to come, you know that. But I have to save my energy for my next chemo treatment."

"Julie, sweetie, we'll be sending you healing energy."

Mark did show up that night for our chakra group. He was a bit more reserved than the week before and offered no psychic revelations.

But he did sit up straighter and paid more attention when we discussed the symptoms of an imbalanced Third Eye Chakra – not trusting one's intuition, migraines, dizziness, indecision. I already knew his extensive experience in these areas so I wanted to offer an especially powerful healing tonight.

"Want more inspiration on what path you should take in life? Want to increase your intuition and psychic abilities?

Let's open the Third Eye Chakra," I said, "the one that gives us insight, premonitions, psychic abilities." Then I read from my Handbook:

"Through the Third Eye Chakra you may connect to the higher self to seek and receive inner guidance. Your psychic and telepathic abilities may be heightened, and you'll be able to trust your inner wisdom."

We did some yoga poses, the Bumble Bee Breath, inhaling deeply then exhaling with the lips vibrating with the sound "hmmmmm." Then we did the Kneeling Yoga Mudra, hands clasped behind us as we tucked our chins toward our chests, bending at the waist and leaning forward until our heads touched the floor. I finished with a guided visualization to open the Third Eye Chakra:

"Breathe in the color indigo, a very dark blue, into the center of your forehead. Here we return to the magic of childhood, to unlimited possibilities, to skills we have always had but which were pushed out of sight. Awaken and clarify your inner vision to have a clear picture of what you want your life to be. Also awaken to a different kind of seeing, clairvoyance or clear sight, that allows you to look inside and beyond the limits of time and space."

After class, Mark, ever the gentleman, helped me straighten the room again. He blew out every candle but one and asked me to show him exactly how to do the heart breath with Julie.

As we started I began trembling a bit and hesitated. Mark got up and brought me my woven white wool shawl, thinking my trembling was from the cool night air. But it was because this breath was the one that Gurudev had taught me and using it brought back a torrent of confusion. Yet I knew that it would be a living link between Mark and Julie.

We sat on the green Indian silk mat with the candle flickering as we breathed deeply, looking into each other's eyes. I soon lost count of my breaths, my attention focused on Mark's eye and heart. I opened my heart and allowed him into the sacred space of my soul, and I became keenly aware that we had been partners before.

I felt myself traveling back to that past life.

Mark is wearing an RAF uniform and an eye patch, and I am in nurse's whites. We have both lost our loved ones, Julie and his brother Richard, and we're clinging to each other. I understood now how our souls were all connected, just picking up where they had left off in the past lifetime. I realized that we reincarnate from life to life with our emotional bodies intact. We carry all the feelings we have ever experienced but not expressed with us from life to life until they finally burst out.

The last flicker of the candle hissed, breaking my trance. I blinked and found myself once again in the dark workshop room. Streaks of dusty light filtered through the window... maybe the light of the moon, or maybe it was just the street light. A Steven Halpern CD played in the background, further setting the scene for magic.

I reached out my hand and Mark took it in both of his. He brought it up to his mouth and tenderly kissed my palm.

We didn't say a word. There was nothing to say. We both loved Julie, and the only way to express it in that moment, truly the only way, was to love each other. Our clothes somehow dissolved, and we, as separate people, just dissolved.

I drew upon all the Tantric knowledge I had ever learned, as if I had learned it for just this night. And the night went on for hours.

As the sun replaced the moonlight in the window, we woke as one body, a unified tangle of four arms, four legs. We completed the circle of love, closing as we had begun. Once again, we kept silent, not a word said. We just stared into each other's eyes, seeing the past, the present, and maybe even the future. Then we dressed, and kissed goodbye.

Healing Past Wrongs

"The heart has its reasons that reason knows nothing of."

~ Blaise Pascal

Threadbar: The next week Mark came to the workshop in Julie's place again. I hadn't heard from either of them. I had practically hidden under the bedcovers all week – I couldn't face what we had done.

Though trying my best to be calm, my hands were shaking when I walked over to Mark and asked, "How's Julie?"

"Same. The chemo is taking its toll and we don't even know if it's helping."

"We'll be working on the Crown Chakra tonight. A perfect time for us to send Julie healing energy." I was too nervous to remember what I wanted to cover, so I read aloud from my Handbook:

"Spiritual oneness is the goal of opening the 7th chakra, the Crown Chakra, the point of knowing and enlightenment. It is our highest energy center, representing liberation, deep understanding, enlightenment and spiritual growth. It represents union with the higher self and the Divine.

"A balanced Crown Chakra brings a profound awakening, a connection to our spiritual nature as well as to cosmic consciousness."

We then did several yoga postures, starting with deep pranayama breathing and ending with the Downward Dog to increase circulation to the Crown Chakra. I told the group to rest in corpse pose as I led them in a Crown Chakra Meditation, finishing with:

"Imagine a rainbow of light pouring down your body, from your Crown Chakra down to your Root Chakra, enveloping you in harmony with everything above and below and around you."

I felt "oneness" come over our group, which included Julie, would always include Julie. I asked them all to direct healing light toward her, to ease her pain, to ease her journey.

I led them in a guided visualization where we pictured Julie in her garden, and fixed anything we saw that could use watering or nurturing in any way. Often you see changes in the physical world after working on the energetic plane.

Mark knocked over a candle as he suddenly got up and ran out of the room. I didn't know what he saw, but I had an eerie feeling that Julie was missing from her garden.

"Let's end with a prayer for Julie," I said, and after a few minutes of silence, we all hugged and took our leave.

I raced to my car, leaving the neighborhood center brightly lit with its door wide open, and ran every stop sign on the way to Julie's condo.

God Speed, Julie

"Wisdom begins at the end."

~ Daniel Webster

"She wasn't here when I got back," Mark said when he opened the door I had nearly banged down.

"What was Julie doing when you left for class?" I asked.

"She said that she needed time alone after the oncologist's call. The news wasn't good," he said. "I could tell by the way Julie smiled so sweetly, so mysteriously, when she hung up the phone. I knew her torture at the hands of the 'enemy,' as she called them, was over. But I didn't know she was going to skip out."

"Have you called her cell?"

"I've called it a thousand times," he yelled, throwing his own phone across the room. Walking over to pick it up, he paused, closed his eyes, and murmured, "She doesn't answer. I even called the police, but they said she's not a missing person for 24 hours."

All she had left behind was a green card next to Mark's computer on her coffee table where he had set up a temporary office to be near her. I picked up the card and read her favorite affirmation, "Life is change, and I make those changes with love and ease."

Just that and her chakra diary nestled into the pillow on the sofa. I turned to the last page, where she had written, *"For me, healing may not be a matter of surviving, but of moving on with a heart full of love, instead of fear, toward my next new adventure."*

"Let's go, she probably went to the ocean, her favorite place," I said, pulling Mark along with me to my car, and then drove like a crazed cabbie to the beach, chanting under my breath to keep from screaming. Mark sat beside me silent as death himself.

I drove to the pier where Julie and I used to surf. Using my sweating, shaking hand to screen the blinding glare of the setting sun, I looked around and saw an old friend, Jocko, stacking rental boards into the back of his rusted-out red truck.

"Have you seen Julie?" Mark and I both asked at the same time.

"Yeah, man, like an hour ago. She gave me 200 clams for my oldest, dinged-up board. Ran into the surf like a bat out of hell. I was gonna stay and watch her stuff man, but hey, it's getting dark and I gotta go, man." He pointed to a pile of clothes on a rock near the shore. We walked over and just collapsed on either side of them. I picked up Julie's wet, wrinkled green shirt and tried to dry my tears with it.

I looked out at the horizon at the tilting and lifting of the sea. The sounds of the ocean battering against the shore were deafening.

Then suddenly it was so quiet. Time had stopped and been put on hold.

I started chanting under my breath, then praying out loud. Then I saw clearly....

"She's swimming with a dolphin," I whispered. "He's guiding her, leading her home."

"God speed," said Mark.

Even though the sun had long ago set, a sparkling glow of all the rainbow's colors appeared above the wind-driven sea. So, she rode a rainbow home!

Regrets Read Out Loud

"We are all visitors to this time, this place. We are just passing through. Our purpose here is to observe, to learn, to grow, to love...and then we return home."

~ Aboriginal Proverb

There was one more week of the Chakra Workshop. I did a chin up out of my grief to go lead the group when every fiber of my soul wanted to curl up and wait for the bad dream to pass and morning to bring a new day. I had let everyone know already about Julie's passing, so it would be a "different" wrap-up than usual.

Mark was the first to show up. He was holding Julie's chakra diary.

"I read it all the way through. She bled on the pages. She gutted herself as much as the chemo did." His voice broke as he said, "Julie wrote on the first page to give it to you, Rebecca, with her love."

So, she had forgiven me?

I thumbed the diary pages silently as the other students found their cushions, afraid that if I began to read it, the tears would come and not stop. We did a silent meditation in honor of Julie. Then, one by one, the group read random excerpts from her diary.

Jean, who Mark helped so much with his energy reading, was the first to take a turn. I was shocked by what Julie had written and even more surprised that Jean would choose this passage, would open this Pandora's Box of our hearts' secrets:

"I knew Rebecca also knew Tantric Sex. Mark's weird squeamishness now made me think he had learned something he shouldn't have. Green may be the color of forgiveness, but it's also the color of envy. Sure, I was jealous of Rebecca's

beauty, her health, her wholeness, while I lay here broken and battered, beautiful no longer. But as the tears exploded down my face, I didn't feel angry. Funny. I actually felt relieved for Mark. He wouldn't be left all alone. I knew now Rebecca would care for him.

"He finally faced me and apologized, 'I needed comforting and she understood. We just got swept away.'

"I asked Mark to show me what Rebecca had taught him. We breathed from his heart into mine and back and before long, yes, more things moved back and forth and the earth moved. Rebecca's not my best friend for nothing."

The whole class gasped at the same time I did. Then Jean passed the book to Tony. He read aloud in his booming, open Throat Chakra voice:

"It's probably a blessing that Mark confessed to sleeping with Rebecca. It's forced me to reflect on love, letting go and forgiveness. I think that is where my healing lies now, on the heart level. I had years of old anger that I had to feel again to release. I thought that anger had given me the strength to leave home and move on in my life. But I know now that it kept poisoning me when I needed to let in love.

"I thought about each thing I was still angry about and felt where it caused me to tense up. Then I relaxed that part of my body, imagining a wave of pure green healing flowing through as I did the Dynamind tapping. Now when I think of my father or the Navy docs or my own mistakes, my body stays relaxed. Without the tension, there's no more anger."

Sarah turned to the end of the diary and read Julie's last few words:

"My body is dripping moisture like at the glistening seashore in Mexico, when I last asked Grandmother Ocean for help, help with the pain, with this unbearable pain. She is calling me home now, while there are no arms to pull me back. No ropes to tie me down on the train tracks where I've lain, by my own choice, and been run over too many times now.

"All I can tell you is to UNTIE your own ropes; throw off any feeling that you didn't do enough, that you're not good enough or can't have what you want; instead, live your life to the fullest; love as much as you can; make your mark on the world while you have the strength to do it!

"I don't have much time, choice or strength left, but with the little I do have, I'm calling a taxi to take me to the ocean. My soul is ready for my next great adventure. I choose to ride a wave there.

"Adios, amigos. I will love you infinitely and eternally."

With her last bit of strength, Julie gave me absolution. But the rest of the group seemed to look at me as if I were guilty of the worst. Or was I just seeing a projection of my own feelings?

We all agreed to gather together for Julie's memorial once I had found her father. And then we said goodbye. Mark was lingering but Jean cried in my arms so long, he left before I could voice another word to him.

Remembering

*"It isn't what you did in the past that will affect the present.
It's what you do in the present that will redeem the past
and thereby change the future."*

~ Paulo Coelho

J ulie's writings from her diary echoed in my head. Whenever I was tempted to grieve, or waste time crying in my pillow (which really couldn't absorb any more tears), I heard her voice:

"Untie your own ropes; throw off any feeling that you didn't do enough, that you're not good enough or can't have what you want; instead, live your life to the fullest; love as much as you can; make your mark on the world."

I wanted the world to benefit from Julie's wisdom and even her mistakes. We alternative healers often don't take advantage of what allopathic medicine can offer – diagnosis and surgery when needed. Other macrobiotic counselors, leaders in the community such as Michio Kuchi's wife and daughter had succumbed to cervical cancer – which they might never have suffered from if they had yearly pap smears. As Julie wrote so wisely, "Complementary medicine is the way to go, taking the best that each discipline has to offer, not being arrogant, like I was, in thinking that you alone know the answer."

I read Julie's diary over and over and decided to publish *The Chakra Diaries** as a tribute to her. The other participants in the workshop were each just as special as Julie and their diaries showed so clearly how a chakra imbalance can lead to everything

* *The Chakra Diaries* is available on Amazon.com.

from homelessness, sex addiction or dysfunction, chronic fatigue, migraines, depression and yes, even energy-sucking spirits. And their diaries showed how balancing the chakras could lead to magic and miracles – the homeless girl became a social worker at a shelter, the sick regained their health, the lonely were now in relationships. It all seemed to come through the healing power of love, the source of all miracles.

Yes, I do believe Julie, her spirit, was healed as well. She had written,

"I know everything that I am going through has come to me for a reason. The most important healing doesn't always occur on the physical level."

I believe she died in peace, triumphing over anger and fear, embracing forgiveness.

But, I still felt guilty, I can't deny it…I had been emotionally attached to Julie getting well, against all odds, and I felt maybe I had failed her. Maybe I hadn't tried hard enough, early enough, often enough to help her. I shouldn't have made love to Mark!

Through all my own therapy sessions and chakra work, I felt I had cut out the poisonous emotional remnants from my disastrous marriage. But a sense of lingering guilt still burned inside me, no matter how I rationalized my choices.

I decided to see the Past-Life Therapist one more time.

He led me down into the depths of my mind with the clicking of his antique clock beating in time with each step I took down, down, into the past. He said, "Go back to the bombed-out hospital. What happens after Julie dies?"

I see the soldier holding my arm as we walk to a cemetery

and put flowers on Julie's grave, then on his brother's grave, marked with Richard's name. Mark and I cling to each other for comfort, but it's clear that he also has to go back to the fight now that his injury is healed. We spend his last evening in London together, comforting each other. He asks me to marry him after the war, but I don't answer, knowing he'll never return from the horror that awaits him.

I jumped up. I also jumped right out of my hypnosis session. But this time, it wasn't out of horror. I finally understood! Mark and I had never had the chance to be together in our last life. I had literally missed the mark thinking Richard was "the one," but he was only a near equivalent. He was only meant to lead me to Mark, to recognize Mark. Our destiny had never been fulfilled. In a flash of insight, I realized there was something too deep and too strong between us for just one incarnation.

The Power of Now

"Do not dwell in the past, do not dream of the future,
concentrate the mind on the present moment."

~ The Buddha

I listened to a chakra meditation tape this morning, journeying up the back of my spine with my breath, focusing on the color and sound of each chakra until I reached the violet Crown Chakra. Though I had listened to this tape many times, it was like I was hearing it for the first time.

"You are returning to stillness, returning to source, to oneness. You are the creator of the cause and the receiver of the effects. Being in the source, you live beyond the traps of time and space, cause and effect. You are free. You move in creative response to what is present in every moment."

I felt it! I felt the oneness. I focused on its essence and saw Julie glowing diamond-white, smiling and sailing smoothly through the clouds, joyous and happy, not held down by earthly concerns or fears, no longer bound by the limits of body and mind. I prayed for compassion, healing, for new possibilities.

Paging through Julie's journal again and again, my finger traced the words she had written with green pencil and wavering letters, "To my teacher and best friend, with love." In other words, she still loved me. Unconditionally.

I often visited Grandmother Ocean, and talked to her like Julie did. And I listened to her answers. Trying to let grief and guilt go, and let love fill its place. I sat by the ocean pier this morning, our pier, and asked again, "Why Julie?" I heard Grandmother Ocean, the wise woman's voice in my head:

"Julie was an angel who helped while she could and left when she had finished her time here. Her soul is on its own path to learn to heal others while she herself remains safe. A lesson she will master. Just like you will master reaching for happiness with no apologies."

I wanted to ask Mark if and when we could ever be together again. But I felt a push-pull going on inside me. We hadn't even had Julie's memorial service yet. After months of looking for Julie's father, I finally located him, got his agreement to fly down from the Bay Area for the service. But the soonest he could do it, he said, was January, five months away!

When I met with Mark to check out spots on the beach to hold the service, memories of our last vigil together at the ocean, at sunset, took my breath away. There were personal, unanswered questions between us, but I couldn't voice them. I silently slipped off my shoes and so did Mark. Wading and walking in the surf, we came to the right spot. A wide stretch of beach, perfect for a ceremonial circle to celebrate Julie's life. A shady pavilion stood just behind on a grassy knoll, ready-made for our memorial meal.

Instead of a kiss when we got back to our cars, I gave him a brochure on a Psychic Healer's workshop. Body scanning, hands-on healing, intuitive counseling. Lots of ways he could learn to use his Third Eye, his psychic powers, to help others.

"Hmm," Mark said. "For all my eyes, I can't see my own future yet." So then, neither could I.

~   ~   ~

Redondo Beach, January 2010

For Julie's memorial service, we picked the evening of the first moon of the new year in the new decade. A palette of pastel pink and purple streaks painted the sky as we tossed the violet orchid blossoms into the ocean in honor of Julie's life. A peek of a rainbow appeared between two puffy cumulous clouds, a brief warning of the downpour that drenched us as we ran to our cars. Our sunset beach picnic overruled by nature, we headed back to where we had begun our Chakra Group, to the community center.

I thought Julie's father and his wife would be joining us for our dinner, but when they drove away from the beach park in the rain I guess they were headed for the airport. Staring into the distant horizon from our circle at the beach, neither of them even blinked as we each said a few words about Julie. Nor did her father say a remembrance of her. Maybe I was wrong that he'd want to know what he'd missed of Julie's life. Maybe there was a reason Julie never called him for help. But he did show up. I think he knew she had forgiven him.

At the community center we set up a fabulous, gourmet macrobiotic feast on the corner tables. But no one was as hungry for food as for consolation. I put out the familiar rainbow-colored Indian silk mats, and we all collapsed comfortably into the regular positions we had taken during the Chakra Workshop.

Mark cleared his throat as loudly as the pop of the champagne he uncorked, and said, "Let's celebrate Julie at her best, in her performance of the Green Power Goddess."

We all sipped our bubbly, getting giddy and giggly as we watched one of Julie's puppet shows he had videotaped a couple years before. The blank gray wall served as a perfect screen for his projected image of the beautiful blond puppeteer guiding her magical marionettes to save the earth and all who lived on her. The kids and parents watching the shows were hooting, hollering and laughing as the Earth Goddess fought off the puppets of environmental destruction – the chemical giant, the pesticide sprayer, the truck spewing grey gusts of carbon dioxide – and saved the endangered wildlife (turtles, polar bears and owls).

When the video was over, Mark brought a huge box holding the puppets from the back of his SUV and said, "Julie left behind not only her marionettes, but so many treasures I'm sure she'd want you all to share."

I stood back, hoping for a meaningful remembrance, but all her puppets, crystals, jewels and books were quickly divided among the other folks in the room, who also loved Julie.

After everyone left I did a final cleanup and walked out of the neighborhood center alone, empty-handed. But in the parking lot, Mark was standing in the light mist of rain talking with another of my students. I waved when Tony got into his bright blue sports car and drove away. Mark and I finally had some time together on this dreary, sad day.

We hugged for what seemed like an hour before he stepped back, lifted up my chin, and kissed away the tears mixed with the drops of rain on my cheeks.

"You know what I'm going to ask again after all these years," he said.

"I do?"

"And I hope you have a better answer now. How about trying one of those macrobiotic restaurants with me on Saturday night?" he asked.

Julie must have approved because, at just that moment, the clouds shifted a bit to the east and the full moon beamed down. I turned again into the comfort of his warm chest, smelled the familiar, delicious citrus scent that exudes from the men I seem destined to love, looked up at the sky, and whispered to Julie, my best friend, now and forever, "Thank you."

A jet passing overhead pierced the sky and my dream-come-true as I remembered, "Oh no, I'm leaving for Hawaii. I have a workshop there in two weeks, but the lava is flowing down to the ocean, a once-in-a-lifetime sight. The Retreat Manager told me to book a flight ASAP, so I did."

"Are you moving to Hawaii again or coming back?" Mark asked as a thunderclap right over our heads sent me scurrying to my car before I could think of the right answer.

He was still standing in the rain when I wiped off my face and rolled down my window and called out, "I don't know, Mark." I hadn't heard from him in four months, had given up hope, made other plans. I wanted to be with Mark, but we never got the timing right! He got into his car as the rain turned into a deluge, and I backed out of the parking lot and headed for home.

I somehow expected him to follow me, so we could talk about this. We needed to talk about this, but no headlights were behind me. My cell phone battery had lost its charge and so had I.

Should I still move to Hawaii as I had planned? Should I alter my life's path for a dinner invitation? Did he want more?

I missed my turn and resorted to the on-ramp for Frustration Highway.

New Beginnings

"Everything comes to us that belongs to us if we create the capacity to receive it."

~ Rabindranath Tagore

My schedule was mind-shattering the following week as I made arrangements to give up the lease on my house, packed up my belongings and shipped everything I would need on the Big Island. I didn't hear from Mark, his cell wasn't accepting any more messages, and his car wasn't parked in front of his condo whenever I took a detour to pass it on my way to UPS.

The longer we went without contact, the more I rationalized that maybe this soft parting was better for both of us. I had always hated goodbyes, and after losing Julie maybe it was just too much. Maybe "Everlasting Love" was a pipe dream from the past.

Anyway, I planned to stay in Hawaii again indefinitely. Paradise was calling me and I could already smell the plumeria blossoms. When I settled into my First Class seat, 3A, on Hawaiian Airlines, and smelled that familiar, intoxicating scent on the elderly Polynesian woman in 3B, I knew I had made the right decision. She looked at me and said, "Won't it be great to get home?" I nodded in agreement.

Once the plane took off and the smog above L.A. was replaced with white billowy clouds, I caught a whiff of citrus. I looked up hoping against hope, having seen too many romantic movies, but it was just the stewardess offering complimentary guava juice as the steward was popping the cork on a bottle of champagne. Of course, it sprayed me with a rush of excruciating memories. Would I ever be with the true love of my life/lives?

After hours of staring out the scratched airplane window at the top of the billowy white clouds, the soothing slack key Hawaiian guitar music finally lulled me to sleep. I needed a few winks after the lost slumber during the nights when I tossed and turned thinking of Mark. Had he just wanted a dinner date or more? Would I ever find out?

I was roughly awoken when the wheels of the plane bumped the runway, and I deplaned still rubbing the sand man out of my groggy eyes, cranky as I usually am when woken from a nap. I followed the crowd in front of me to baggage claim, only to find my overly-stuffed suitcase spilled open, going round and round on the luggage carousel. I quickly tried to gather up all my private articles (like the world could see my private heartache) as they sped by me on the endlessly circling carousel. When I finally packed them back up, I pulled the overweight bag out to the Hilo airport curb smack into the wall of 100% humidity that I had for-gotten about when I dreamed of Hawaii. Another smack in the face was the absence of the Retreat Center van that was supposed to pick me up.

Pulling out my cell to call the Center, I jumped back from the curb when a muddy convertible jeep suddenly screeched to a stop in front of me, beeping so loudly I knew it must be a rental. "Jerk," I whispered under my breath as I dialed the Resort Center. But the horn kept honking. Don't they know it's not considered very aloha to honk your horn in Hawaii? But this tourist in the goofy tied-under-the-chin sun hat was definitely full of aloha as he got out of the rental car and put a yellow and white plumeria lei around my neck.

"Mark, how did you ever...." My question was stopped with a kiss.

"What took you so long? I thought you were leaving the next day, so I've been here since Wednesday. I told the van driver I would handle this pickup."

~   ~   ~

It was Saturday night and we were having a vegan dinner together after all – at the Center's buffet. In between our thorough chews, I poured out my secrets...the whole story. From Richard and his resemblance to Mark, to the point of his attracting me and frightening me at the same time, to my explosive dreams, past lives, loss, grief and guilt. He knew some of the details and, of course, felt the same loss and grief I did over losing Julie. But I had the exclusive on guilt, my lifelong companion.

At sundown, we hiked with headlights over the jagged, black lava rock to watch the new flow explode into the ocean. I held Mark's hand to steady myself both physically and emotionally while I listened to his secrets. How he had fallen in love with me at first sight yet accepted my rejection when he realized that part of his destiny was to help Julie.

Mark had seen a "darkness" in her leg long before Julie's diagnosis, had told her to be careful, to check it out. When they learned of her melanoma, his psychic powers scared him but also awakened something of the medical intuitive and healer in him.

"I loved Julie," he said. "I'll always love her. I know it was right for me to be with her. But God help me, I can finally say it – I've always ached for you. I've waited and waited; now it's our time."

We arrived at the site where the burning red hot lava was traveling down the mountain from the crater to the ocean, creating an explosion of new life as it hardened into new land at the edge of the bright blue sea. I hoped we could forge a new life out of the explosive disasters of the past.

The lava entering the sea burst into a rainbow of colors that drew us forward, while the heat pushed us back... the push-pull I had always felt with Mark. I clung to his hand as we walked back across the ups and downs of the jagged lava field to our car, and we shared more of the ups and downs of our lives, more of the unspoken words we'd held back during the last decade of our lives.

When we reached my cottage, next door to the one he had chosen, I invited him in and we snuggled on the comfy futon bed and talked through the night. Not just talked. More than once we released our pent-up passion, not in a slow, tantric way, but with urgent, scorching sex that was just as sacred.

As the sky brightened outside the cottage windows, Mark suggested a sunrise swim at the beach just below the cliffs. We were the first people that day to hike the steep path down to the secluded bay fronted with black pebbly sand.

The graceful curves of the leaping spinner dolphins were silhouetted against the rising yellow ball of light. These amazing creatures played, jumped and spun about a half mile out in the bay. I had enjoyed them up close before so I decided to sit (or rather lie) this one out on my pareo to watch the show, but Mark ran right into the crashing surf for his first chance to swim with dolphins.

My sleepy eyes were startled open by falling pine needles from the windswept ironwood trees lining the shore. I sat up looking for Mark. Way, way out in the water I saw the blue snorkel tube attached to his mask rising and falling between waves, the ocean's as well as his. I thought he was waving hello, but I soon realized it was a call for help. I knew he must be caught in the notorious rip tide, unable to swim back toward the shore.

The beach was still empty, no help in sight but a discarded old surf board leaning against the scraggly tree holding tightly to the water's edge. Thanking Julie once again, this time for teaching me to surf, I quickly jumped on the board and paddled toward Mark. The current pushed me south, closer and closer toward the cliff of dangerous black lava rocks as I struggled to reach him.

The questions raced through my mind like an old-time newsreel. Were we to join Julie? Was our karma catching up with us? Was our short time together all we would have in this life?

Out of breath, but summoning energy from the now-bright sun, I finally reached a weary Mark and pulled him onto the board just as he was about to go down for the hundredth time. After endless minutes of fighting the power of the current, I rode one of Grandmother Ocean's largest waves back to the safety of the shore with the love of my life.

Mark coughed up a gallon of sea water onto the black sand, then laid his head in my lap. He looked up at me and when he could finally catch his breath, said, "You saved me."

I did. I really did. In this lifetime, I really did.

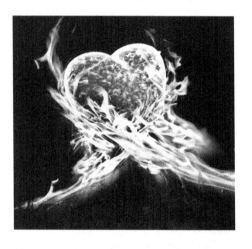

"Love never dies, it is the light that reunites us from lifetime to lifetime."

~ Rumi

PART II

Using Chakra Healing on Your Path

"The past is over and done with... fill your mind with awareness of the beauty and goodness in the present."

~ Serge Kahili King, Ph.D.

BALANCE YOUR CHAKRAS, BALANCE YOUR LIFE has become my theme song, my mantra. My life may have been more or less tumultuous than yours, but we all face imbalances in our energy centers that can be healed.

I've decided to be happy, plain and simple. I believe that everyone, regardless of the circumstances, can choose to be happy. It is always waiting in the wings, ready to join us on cue. Just like love. And forgiveness.

To choose happiness, I believe you have to choose balance. Rather than a crash diet to lose weight, then seesaw back up again, choose a balanced diet consisting of whole foods, such as Macrobiotics. And balance your busy day of stressful activities with yoga, meditation and deep breathing. These practices have helped me and so many others maintain balance in the face of everyday storms and struggles.

It also helps to have an "instant healing" technique you can use to balance your emotional, mental, physical and spiritual bodies – which are all connected to your chakras. That's why I want you to experience Dynamind!

When I met Serge Kahili King, Ph.D., a Hawaiian-trained shaman and teacher of the ancient Huna philosophy, he taught me the Dynamind Process. In Hawaiian, Huna means "secret" and Dynamind is the ultimate healing secret to balancing your life in just minutes a day.

Whether you experience pain, illness or stress, or just want to enhance your energy, you'll want to learn and practice this simple-yet-profound technique.

According to the ancient Huna philosophy, all dis-ease is caused by stress. Or rather, the tension we hold in our bodies in reaction to stress. So, all Huna healing techniques have one purpose – to release tension, and allow the body's healing energy to flow beautifully and unrestricted. Once the tension that is blocking them is removed, the chakras can open and spin in their bright rainbow colors, and the bodily functions and emotional states associated with them will move into balance as well.

Dynamind is a quick and effective exercise, documented in Dr. King's book, *Healing for the Millions*. This quick and easy technique can virtually be used anywhere, anytime and often has deeply transformative results. Now, with his help, I've applied the process to Chakra Healing.

So, How Do You Start?

It's a good idea to set your intention every day with a ritual. I use Dynamind each morning, after I scan my body, mind and emotions and see what I'd like to change and what I'd like to manifest. Then, I use Dynamind.

I use it when I'm off track, when I'm stuck, when I'm feeling negative, disconnected, or just out of sorts. I also use it when I'm feeling positive and want to access or sustain more joy and bliss by doing a Dynamind Toner.

All chakra imbalances manifest in uncomfortable physical and emotional problems that you can describe as a "feeling." Dr. King advises asking yourself what emotion is a problem and where you feel that emotion in the body. Then you can work on changing that physical sensation to let the healing energy of the body flow freely.

Our energy centers affect our emotions and "feelings" in our physical bodies, just as our emotions and feelings can disrupt the balance of our chakras.

Here's how this played out in my story, as I moved through the course of heartache, guilt, depression, loss, and grief, into the light.

My Root Chakra, the seat of financial and emotional safety and security, became unbalanced when I found myself feeling alone and insecure – having moved to Los Angeles, finding no work as an actress, and losing my husband's attention. I was far from family and support of any kind, found myself growing more and more insecure, jealous, and soothing myself with fattening foods.

My Sacral Chakra, the center of sexuality, creativity and relationships, crashed after I felt abandoned by my guru, the man I saw as my spiritual savior, the man who taught me to raise my kundalini energy. But what can open, can also close. Trauma, like the emotional grief and guilt I felt over my husband's death, multiplied by what I felt was the betrayal by Gurudev, closed my Sacral Chakra down tight. Years later, after a love affair with promiscuity led to the opposite extreme of celibacy, I was diagnosed with an ovarian cyst, related to a Sacral Chakra imbalance.

Starting on my new path as a yoga instructor, I didn't have the self-confidence to open my own studio, to position myself as a leader. My Solar Plexus Chakra, the focal point of our identity, self-esteem and vitality, how we assert our personal power, take risks and make decisions, was weak and constricted. Even though I knew that the wounded healer can be the best example for others, I felt inadequate. By balancing my Solar Plexus Chakra, I basked in newfound power and the confidence to create my own studio, Open Heart Yoga, and teach Chakra Balancing Workshops.

If you've lived life, you've probably also experienced rejection in your relationships, perhaps sorrow and, perhaps, like me, guilt as well. How do you open your heart again? After what I felt was the last betrayal I could bear, my foray into Tantric Sex at the Hawaiian Retreat Center which left me feeling abandoned and angry at my partner for straying, the many heartbreaks during my life bubbled to the surface and my Heart Chakra shut down. My back tightened, I blamed both my partners and myself, and didn't think I could ever open to the healing power of love again. I was blasted by the issues commonly associated with the Heart Chakra, including anger, resentment, jealousy, possessiveness, lasting grief, depression, and upper back and shoulder pain − I felt them all. Thankfully, Serge Kahili King taught me the Dynamind Process and I let these "feelings" go finally.

Keeping secrets, such as my past life issues with Julie and Mark, inhibited my Throat Chakra, the focal point of sound, communication and self-expression. My Throat Chakra was out of balance, making me less than effective as a teacher and a friend, because I wasn't sharing my truth. I don't think my Throat Chakra truly became as strong as it could be until I strengthened it and was able to tell Mark my many secrets, from this life and our past life together.

Mark is an example of a person who had Third Eye Chakra issues most of his life. While he was gifted with extraordinary psychic powers, he pushed them down, devalued them, didn't use them to help others. Julie's illness and death forced us both to recognize our Third Eye Chakra imbalances and to develop our Third Eye centers to gain the connection we needed, the inspiration we needed, to go on with our lives. While I may never have the psychic abilities Mark is gifted with, opening my Third Eye has enabled me to see beyond my limited mind and open myself to answers from my higher self, the Divine represented in nature for me as Grandmother Ocean, and my angels and spirit guides.

After my best friend died, all my energy centers were affected, but I recognized these emotional or mental health issues commonly associated with the Crown Chakra – a feeling of aloneness, depression, and a loss of meaning. I meditated on the Crown Chakra for Divine help. Concentrating on the Crown Chakra using Dynamind gave me a connection to Julie's spirit, and a deep connection to universal love, wisdom and forgiveness.

~   ~   ~

I have now learned to balance these chakra centers by healing my physical and emotional problems using Dynamind...and you can too.

Chakra energy centers hold a vibration and color, like a human rainbow, and are affected by every experience, thought, and emotion we have ever had. You can use that vibration and color to enhance the Dynamind Process... follow along with me in the example here, and learn how I've applied Dynamind to all seven chakras in my book *Balance your Chakras, Balance your Life with Dynamind* and the accompanying *Balance and Tone your Chakras* video.

How to Use Dynamind:

1) FOCUS: Hold your hands in a loose prayer-like position.

2) DECLARE: Make a statement that acknowledges the problem, creates a positive expectation, and expresses the outcome you want, e.g., *"I feel guilt tightening my chest, and that can change. I want that feeling to go away."*

3) RELEASE: Tap 7 times on four power spots. First, the Heart Center.

Then, tap 7 times on the web between the thumb and first finger of each hand, first your left...

Then, tap 7 times on the web between the thumb and first finger of your right hand...

Then, tap 7 times on the back of the neck, on the top bone of your spine (the 7th cervical vertebra)...

4) BREATHE: Finish with a deep breath, inhaling with your attention at the top of your head...

Exhale with your attention at the bottom of your feet.

See how easy it is? Just say your problem out loud, declare it can change, and that you want the pain or problem to go away. In this way, you can direct your subconscious to change negative patterns. Tap 7 times on four key power spots on the body, and finish with a deep breath. This should release the tension in your body associated with the problem and let your body's energy flow freely again.

If you finish the Dynamind Process and still feel pain or tension, repeat the exercise until you feel a release. It can help to add in a symbol before you do the tapping. In my example, of tightening in my chest, I imagined a fist squeezing my heart and then visualized the fist opening and green love light flowing in. Or you can visualize the chakra in its brilliant rainbow color spinning in a clockwise direction. Instead of tapping, you can hum while you touch the four power spots – using mantras or tones associated with each chakra – which is also very effective.

The real secret to success with Dynamind is working through the layers. On your first try, you may just say, *"I feel tightness in my back and that can change. I want that feeling to go away."*

But if you don't feel complete relief, add in the emotion that may be causing the discomfort, like I did, saying, *"I feel guilt tightening my chest, and that can change. I want that feeling to go away."*

Like peeling the layers of an onion, you may feel the pain moving through your body to a different area, or a lessening of intensity of the pain – that's great! It means you're moving energy and, if you continue the process, you will succeed in releasing the tension that is throwing you off balance.

~   ~   ~

To learn how to apply Dynamind to balance all seven chakras, and to strengthen them each day with Dynamind Toners, see *Balance your Chakras, Balance your Life with Dynamind* and the accompanying *Balance and Tone your Chakras* video at www.TheChakras.org.

For a free booklet on Dynamind and more information on Serge Kahili King and his organization, go to www.Huna.org/html/dmind.html.

Acknowledgements

I'd like to thank the many teachers who have appeared on my path. I would especially like to thank Serge Kahili King, Ph.D., who has guided me in my own healing, and teaches and shares the Huna philosophy around the world through Aloha International.

For help with my story, I'd like to express thanks to my beta readers and editors, especially Roger Harris of IndieAuthorCounsel.com, who inspired me to keep on, keeping on, sharing my deepest secrets.

And to you, my readers, who have given me your time and your ear... many blessings on your path.

Namaste!

Becca Chopra

About the Author

Becca Chopra is a holistic counselor, yoga and meditation instructor, and writer. Read the full stories of Julie, Mark and the other chakra workshop participants as they conquer their demons and reach for their dreams in *The Chakra Diaries*.

If you'd like to *Balance your Chakras, Balance your Life with Dynamind*, please check out Becca's new book and accompanying DVD.

For more information on Becca Chopra's work, and previews of her upcoming book on Chakra Healing, visit: www.TheChakras.org.

Made in the USA
Monee, IL
04 March 2021